ALSO BY SANDRA BENÍTEZ

Bitter Grounds

A Place Where the Sea Remembers

the weight of all things

the
weight
of all
things

Sandra Benítez

HYPERION

New York

Library of Congress Cataloging-in-Publication Data

Benítez, Sandra.
The Weight of All Things / Sandra Benítez.—1st ed.
p. cm.
ISBN 0-7868-6399-4
1. El Salvador—History—1979–1992—Fiction. 2. Romero, Oscar
A. (Oscar Arnulfo), 1917–1980—Death and burial—
Fiction. 3. Massacres—El Salvador—History—20th
century—Fiction. I. Title.

PS3552.E5443 R58 2000
813'.54—dc21
99-051759

PAPERBACK ISBN 0-7868-8703-6

Book design by Christine Weathersbee

FIRST PAPERBACK EDITION

10 9 8 7 6 5 4 3 2 1

For
Christopher Charles Title
Jonathon James Title
Finer sons no mother could have

"Life is heavier than the weight of all things."

Rilke

A HISTORICAL NOTE

Two events detailed in this novel are based on actual occurrences that took place in El Salvador:

March 30, 1980—More than 80,000 people gathered in and around the Metropolitan Cathedral for the funeral of Arch bishop Oscar Arnulfo Romero, who was assassinated on March 24 while celebrating mass. Thirty-five were killed and 450 were wounded after explosions and shooting caused the crowd to panic.

May 14, 1980—Six hundred campesinos fleeing rural repression were massacred at the Sumpul River by Salvadoran and Honduran troops.

one

Later, after the bombs went off, after the monstrous black clouds they sent up dissipated in the gentle breeze, after the shooters, whoever they might have been, pocketed their stubby handguns and vanished into the crowd, after the police ceased returning fire and attempted instead, with their superior presence, to control a multitude run amuck, it would be clear it was a bullet to the head that killed her.

But for now, she was alive. Until the shooting, the crowd had filled the cathedral to overflowing; it had backed up against the doors, spilled down the broad steps and out into the plaza, where tens of thousands of El Salvador's faithful drove elbows and shoulders into each other, where but a dozen held umbrellas over their heads as a hedge against the sun, and the majority stood acceptingly in the heat, sweat staining half-moons under their arms and triangles over their breastbones. Everywhere there was the stale odor of humanity pressed together in mourning.

Because she and the boy had come early, she had won for them a coveted spot: they stood against the iron-railed barricade separating the general crowd from the cathedral doors and from Archbishop Romero's casket, positioned there, plain and unadorned, on the landing above the steps. The casket gleamed in the noonday sun. It rested beneath a banner draped over the church entrance, a banner imprinted with Monseñor's beloved bulldogish face.

When the bombs went off, the solemn silence maintained by the multitude was debased by shouts and cries pitched high with surprise and then with terror. When the *pakpakpak!* of pistols started up, the *brrrttt!* of automatic weapons began, the crowd broke apart and scrambled for cover. She and the boy were pressed instantly against the barricade, but she held his arm in a fierce grip lest the swell and sway of the people sweep him from her. She tried scrambling over the barricade because it was only waist-high; she thought they both could make it, but there were people jammed against the other side, too. Bullets whizzed by from both directions. Because he was not a husky boy and there was only so much they could do against the riptide of the people, he folded at her feet, his slender back against the barricade.

She used rapid blows from her elbows to gouge a space around him. She dropped down upon him, draping herself over him as if she were a truce flag. She did it because she was his mother. She did it because just yesterday she had gone to fetch him from Chalatenango, the region to the north where he lived with his grandfather; because this morning she had brought him on the bus to San Salvador, a dangerous journey over guerrilla-held land, but a necessary journey if her son were someday to state "When I was nine I attended the funeral of a martyred saint."

She spoke directly into her son's ear, her words vying with the madness surrounding them: "I am here, Nicolás," she said, struggling to keep hysteria at bay. She did not know if he could hear her, but she continued nonetheless. "Do not fear. La Virgen is with us. Monseñor is with us, too." The archbishop, newly dead, his body only meters away and not yet a statue in a niche, and already she was petitioning him for a miracle. She turned her head a bit to get a sense of things: the railings of the barricade were like prison bars. How long had she and the boy been tucked in this position? How long since a shoe had been torn off her foot? How many people had trampled her back, used her as a stepping stool to vault over the barricade? A bullet caromed near, so close the impact of it hitting the railing reverberated in her ears. She pressed her cheek once more against her son's, sought to spread herself more completely over him. "Holy Mother, protect us," she uttered.

Nicolás strained to decipher the sound of his mother's prayers. He was now lying on his side where he had tilted over, both legs drawn up to his chest, arms holding his canvas backpack against himself. He felt the soft pressing weight of his mother, her arms cradling his head, her words one hot breath after another against his cheek. The smell of her was like sweet damp earth. He imagined himself away from here. Imagined himself back home, inside the cave he had found carved into one of the hills behind his rancho. In his secret place he was confined like this, encaved, but it was a condition that brought him comfort. His cave was shadowy, but the shadows did not frighten him. On the contrary; shadows and even the deep dark were an advantage over the light of broad day, the light that could expose you and point you out as accusingly as a finger.

He heard his mother murmuring, repeating and repeating a simple prayerful phrase: "Santa María, Madre de Diós."

The Lord is with you, he responded, but in his head, where it was best to pray.

When the bullet found its mark, the impact caused her

arms to flail upward for an instant before they flopped down. Nicolás felt the weight of her push suddenly against him and then he felt her go limp. "Mamá," he said, and it was like an imploration.

Years later, when he was much older and he truly understood, when he was called to give an account of what he had lived through, he would say, "Like water pouring over stone, that is how she slipped away from me."

two

Nicolás lay still as a tomb. If life were such that he would never have to move again, the fact would please him. He did not know, would never know, that the bullet that entered his mother's skull traveled directly down the middle of her head and lodged deep in her belly, where it lost its momentum. These things would be discovered later in the makeshift morgue teeming with doctors working over the bodies the Green Cross volunteers had lifted from the plaza and thrown over their shoulders like so many coffee sacks.

Lying tucked in the consoling shadows beneath his mother, Nicolás allowed his mind to wander, to disregard the acridness of smoke still lingering after the explosions, the sound of stampeding feet, many of them shoeless now, slapping against the concrete of the plaza. The sound reminded him of someone making a tortilla. The *slapslapslap* of corn dough turning against a palm. Other than this sound and the occasional shout of discovery, the plaza had gone menacingly calm. Something sour and thick rose in his throat, and he swallowed it back, wishing he had a tortilla to help him do it. There were five colones tucked into the side of his work boots; his grandfather had provided two bills for the trip, and the rest his mother had handed over just after they had stepped off the bus at the terminal. Five colones would get him plenty of tortillas. He had seen the food stands in a market they had walked past on the way to the cathedral. He had wanted to stop and eat. He would pay, he had told her, but his mother had pulled him along. No time for that now, she had said. And now here they were, and his stomach was empty.

Footsteps approached, these feet shod and wearing something sturdy. "Let's tend to this one," a voice said, then his mother was lifted from him and a flood of sunlight gave him away. "My God! Take a look at this!" another voice exclaimed, and Nicolás threw his hands up over his head in protection.

"It's a boy," the one said.

"He's alive," a voice trailed after.

A shadow fell between Nicolás and the sun. A man squatting down beside him had caused it. He wore a white helmet with a big green cross above the visor. "Have you been hit?" he asked.

Nicolás shook his head. He raised himself up and looked around for his mother. The second man, helmeted like the first, had hooked his hands under her armpits and was dragging her away. As he hauled her off, she facedown and listless, her one shoe scraped over the rough surface of the plaza. Soon the shoe fell off, and Nicolás got quickly to his feet and rushed to retrieve it. His legs were cramped and trembling. "That's my mother," Nicolás said. "I think she fainted." He shook the weakness from his legs, then stooped to pluck up the black, flat-soled shoe. It looked like a broad little boat, one he might set to bob on the river. Nicolás pointed the shoe toward his mother. "Her name is Lety Veras," he said, as if speaking her name were proof of some kind. He slipped the shoe into his backpack and hooked the pack over his shoulders. He steadied himself against the barricade, keeping his eyes on his mother, on the way the two men now carried her between them. "Where are you taking her?" he asked, trying to keep fright from his voice. He was nine, after all, and a man.

"Into the cathedral," the one man said, pointing with his chin up the steps in its direction. "It's still too dangerous out here."

Nicolás turned around. As if they had been tossed from a fast-moving truck, papers and placards were strewn on the ground. Bags and shoes were bunched into mounds like accumulated refuse. Dozens of people were being moved toward the church: some slung over shoulders, some dragged along the ground, others carried as limp as hammocks between pairs of volunteers. To provide cover for those who risked their lives, men from populist organizations lay belly-down around the plaza. Propped up on their elbows, they aimed their pistols this way and that, but they no longer fired.

A clump of shoes lay directly in Nicolás's path. With the toe of his boot, he hastily poked through it. He would find his mother's second shoe. She would be grateful, for what good would one be without the other? But after a moment he abandoned the effort, for most of the shoes were black. They all looked like little boats to him. Nicolás sprinted to catch up to the men who now carried his mother through the cathedral doorway, only a dozen paces away. When he reached the church's bottom steps, a line of policemen materialized at the top of them. They stepped in front of the door and cordoned off the entrance. "No admittance!" one pronounced, lifting up a hand that seemed as large as a stop sign.

"My mother's in there!" Nicolás cried out. "Two men with green crosses just carried her in!" Nicolás hurled himself against the mountain towering before him, but the man grasped his rifle like a butting ram and drove Nicolás back. "No admittance!" he bellowed again. Others, too, were being turned away.

Behind the line of policemen, the wide cathedral doors were a yawning mouth that had swallowed up his mother.

Nicolás ran off to the side of the church. He found an unguarded entrance, pulled the heavy door half open, and slipped inside. New chaos greeted him. The church was glutted with people: those who had been under its roof when the shooting began and those who had managed to flee the plaza and find refuge within its walls. Inside, the people railed against fate, against authority, against even their brothers.

Nicolás shoved his way through the throng. He pushed toward the place near the front doors where he'd last seen his mother. Breaking into an open space, he caught a glimpse of two men with green crosses and the limp woman they dragged between them. Relief flooded Nicolás, but when he came close he saw that she had gray hair knotted at the back of her neck. He turned away. Where was his mother?

The redolence of incense rising from the altars stung his nostrils and turned his empty stomach. It blended with the odor of hot wax burning in the votives, and these commingled with the stench of a multitude fearing for their lives. In the church, photojournalists abounded. Startling flashes from their cameras recorded everything. Nicolás's vision swam now with the sight of openmouthed, bloodied bodies lying on the floor, one against the other like fallen logs. He circled the spots where they lay, his heart in his mouth at the thought that his mother might be there among them. As he searched, his ears began to hum. It was like the one and only time he had been to the sea. He had been swimming with his mother when a rogue wave had caught him unawares, tumbling him round and round, abrading his skin with sea sand and filling his mouth with salt. His mother had rescued him. His mother had snatched him up out of the surf and pressed him against her bright yellow bathing suit while he sputtered and coughed and fought to find his breath. "My boy's all right," she had said. "Your mother's got you now."

Now it was his turn to rescue her. He must reach out and pluck her from this sea of churning people. He searched every aisle, shouldering his way through the people who shoved back. He inspected every crowded niche. Shouting above the din, he asked questions of those who appeared to be people who might know the answers: "I am looking for my mother. The men with the green crosses brought her in. Where could my mother be?"

His questions were answered by a single, simple question in return: "Was your mother wounded?" When he hesitated to respond, a hesitation due in part to the fact that he had seen no blood—and how could there be wounds when there wasn't any blood?—sad expressions flitted across faces, and then those showing sadness simply turned away.

In the end, he approached a priest, because from priests you get the truth. He tugged on el padre's white cassock and asked a different kind of question: "Where are the wounded taken?"

"Look around you," the priest said. "The dead are all around." He pointed at places where the bodies were lined up.

"No," Nicolás said, shaking his head vigorously. "Not the dead. The wounded. Where are the wounded taken?"

"To the hospital," the priest said.

He would go, then, to the hospital. When he found her there, miraculously unharmed and incredulous herself at the events that had transpired, he would hang on to her so tightly she would be incapable of ever leaving him again.

three

He left the cathedral through the side door. He walked away from the plaza down a street he recognized. He recalled the tiny corner store, the one selling images of saints and of Jesús. His mother had pointed to a framed picture of la Virgen Milagrosa, the Miraculous Virgin that hung by a cord from the meshed-wire door. His mother was especially devoted to la Virgen and had even named him after her. Nicolás de la Virgen Veras was his name in full. To mark the honor, Nicolás wore a chain around his neck with an oval medal stamped with la Virgen's image. On sight of the picture, Lety Veras had signed herself, a quick brown thumb against her forehead and mouth. She gave Nicolás a look and he had crossed himself, too. Now the store was shuttered and who knew where la Virgen had gone. Though it was but early afternoon, most of the shop owners had pulled down their corrugated iron doors and there were few shoppers on the streets. Nicolás thrust his hands deep into his pockets and leaned ahead as if walking into a stiff wind. He had hooked one strap of his backpack over a shoulder, and the bag, weighted by his mother's shoe and his other possessions, bumped against him as he went.

Though he was bound for the hospital, wherever that might be, he first needed something in his stomach. He entered the first open eating place he found. Inside, a few people sat at long tables; a large woman, clearly the owner and surely the grandmother of many, deftly turned browning tortillas over on the pottery griddle spanning a bed of glowing coals. Sooty clay pots sat directly on the embers, pots filled with softening black beans and with chicken broth spiced with leaves of chipilín. Emitting its own delicious aroma, a pot of coffee simmered next to the soup.

Nicolás used a piece of tortilla to scrape up his beans. Handing over an extra fifteen cents, he treated himself to a slice of hard cheese. This he crumbled, savoring the pungent taste of it. Up in the mountains where he and his grandfather lived, cheese was a rarity. Now that the war had started in earnest, there was not much of anything. Only tortillas and beans. Once or twice a week an egg from the hen. She laid one every day, of course, but given the situation, eggs were a precious commodity that could be used for bartering.

The grandmother approached him. "Do you want more coffee, Chele?" She called him *Chele*, which was an adjective for "fair one." He was light-skinned, it was true; he had tea-colored eyes like his mother and her mother as well. There were many in his region who were fair of skin and pale of eyes. In school, he had learned the reason for this, how years and years ago the Nahuat region of Chalatenango had been populated by a white-skinned race from across the sea. The Conquest, the teacher called it, and the word sounded evil in her mouth.

Nicolás shrugged about the coffee, which meant he wanted some. About being called Chele, he said nothing, something he usually did when people called him that. She picked up his mug and took it over to the pot and ladled him a second filling. When she set the mug down, she plopped herself down across from him. He looked up at her from his beans, thinking it surely wasn't at him that she was directing her attention. But he was wrong.

"It's not safe to be out," she said matter-of-factly. She propped her large shelf of a bosom on the table as if giving it a rest. "Tell me, where do you live?"

"In Chalate," he said, which was a way of saying Chalatenango. "I live with my grandfather."

"¡Uy!" she exclaimed. "It's dangerous up there."

"Sí," he said, because he wished to be polite. If his mother were here and she caught him shrugging again, she would give him an elbow.

"What are you doing down here?"

"I came to see the funeral mass."

"You came alone?"

He shook his head. "I came with my mother. She went up to Chalate and brought me back. My mother loves el Monseñor."

"Where's your mother now?"

Nicolás hesitated, because not actually knowing his mother's whereabouts made it impossible for him to answer. Instead, he shrugged again, feeling this time he was justified.

The grandmother lowered her head in thought, and Nicolás went back to shoveling beans into his mouth with his tortilla. He now could feel her eyes upon him again, but he did not look up to see if this was so. "Does your mother live here in the capital?" she asked at length.

Nicolás nodded. "She works here," he said. "She's a nursemaid for the family of Don Enrique and la niña Flor."

"This family, what's their last name?"

"I don't know." The fact dismayed him, but he had never heard the name, had not paid attention even if it had been spoken. When his mother came to visit, when she wrote him letters, it was always "la niña Flor" this and "el don Enrique" that.

"Where do they live?"

"Up in some neighborhood." That he didn't know even this was like a rogue wave coming at him again. He took a swig of coffee and then another, using the rich strong taste to brace himself for the question he had to ask. He wiped his mouth with the back of his hand. "Can you tell me where the hospital is?"

She herself shrugged, a movement that briefly raised her bosom from the table before she lowered it again. "There are many hospitals," she said. "Which one do you mean?"

"The one where they take those wounded at the cathedral."

Her parrotlike eyes burrowed in at him, and he averted his gaze from her stare. He crumbled the last of his cheese onto the last of his beans, washed this and the end of his tortilla down with what remained of his coffee. He had to swallow hard to get it all down.

"Did something happen to your mother? Did something happen at the cathedral?"

In answer he took a swipe at his mouth again.

"Was your mother shot?" she asked.

Nicolás felt once more the pressing slump of his mother's sheltering body.

"Was your mother killed?" the grandmother went on.

Nicolás's ears began to ring again. He jumped up from the table and rushed out into the street, his backpack in hand. He couldn't bear to be in a place where the words *mother* and *killed* had been spoken together and hovered like threats in the air. With tears in his eyes, he started to run, his boots making dull sounds along the sidewalk. For a minute or two he thought the food stand owner might be behind him, but when he glanced back nobody was there. He went a few blocks, and the dome of the cathedral loomed and the church rose like an omen before him. He decided to go back. Start again where he had last seen his mother. That was where he belonged.

• • •

Compared to what he had earlier seen, an enigmatic silence now prevailed inside the church. Though soldiers were posted along the front steps and around the perimeter of the plaza, he had no trouble entering. He passed through one of the side doors and found some people kneeling in the pews, others milling aimlessly in the aisles, but they were few compared to the multitude of hours before. All the bodies had been removed—Monseñor's casket, too. The wide front doors of the cathedral were closed, and the candles glowing in the niches and at the main and side altars flickered his shadow on the floor as he passed them. He spent an hour retracing his steps in search of his mother. As he went along, he muttered a little prayer to himself about finding her. If she were not in the church, she might be at Don Enrique's and la niña Flor's. It was on this bright possibility that he focused. His mother opening the door of a rich family's house. His mother's surprise when she saw him again. There you are! she would exclaim. I looked everywhere for you.

Now night had fallen, and he was half sitting in the middle of one of the back pews in an out-of-the-way spot, steeped in shadow. On the wall not far from him, a candle in a tall red glass nestled inside a wall sconce lighted up a painting of la Virgen Milagrosa. She was dressed in a white robe and had a long creamy veil. A blue cloak covered her robe. Upon her head sat a tall golden crown; from her outstretched hands silver rays of light emanated. He took it as a second omen. The image of Our Miraculous Mother looking his way. In the little church back home a wall niche held a small wooden statue of the same saint. When his mother visited, and before the church was closed up and they could still go to mass, she would march him up to the statue and light a votive under it. "Pray to la Virgencita, Nico," she said to him. "She's your mother, too."

Nicolás de la Virgen Veras knew that this was true. He knew it because while he sat there in Our Lady's presence a plan had come to him. In the morning he would board the bus to Chalatenango and then go on to El Retorno, his village. Once home, he would collect one of his mother's letters, learn from the envelope where Don Enrique and la niña Flor lived. He would come back to his mother then. Surprise her with her shoe. But for tonight he would make the pew his bed, curl up and try to sleep under the watchful, chinablue gaze of his second mother.

four

At six o'clock, when the sky was pinking up, Nicolás boarded the number 38 bus to Chalatenango, a big, wide vehicle with a side stack that spouted clouds of diesel smoke. He sat on a narrow banquette covered with cracked green vinyl. The backrest was pitched permanently forward, which made sitting uncomfortable. He chose the seat deliberately; he wished to ride beside an old woman who was slumped next to the window. All the old women in the world seemed to be related; all had wizened faces, gray wiry hair, and heads and shoulders swathed in thin tapados. They all lived their lives keeping their own counsel, making it a rule to never look a stranger in the eye. Nicolás thought it was wise to seek out such old ones, even though hardly a word might pass between them. Young people, specifically young men, provided dangerous company. Too frequently they were dragged from buses, from eating places, even from the sanctity of their own dwellings, by the soldiers of el Ejercito Nacional, the National Army. As they strutted grandly about in their camouflaged uniforms with their blousey trouser legs tucked into their boot tops, they shouldered assault rifles that they did

17

not hesitate to use if their suspicions were overly aroused. Other times, the threat came from paramilitary squads, men in brown khaki uniforms and round-visored caps, equally fortified with gun power, storm troopers who flung out capture nets and undertook inquisitions. And over all else was the abiding presence of the National Police, the Treasury Police, and the National Guard, all with rounded steel helmets and chin straps, all armed with rifles and a perplexing hatred for their own brothers.

Caught between their guns were the people, the ordinary people for whose supposed benefit the war was being waged. On one side was the right, claiming it fought against the tyranny of communism. On the other side, the left, struggling, it said, against the injustice of oligarchs and militarists. But while the two sides fought for their principles, most of the dying was done by the people.

Since the war had begun in earnest about a year ago, normality had been leeched by alarming degrees from Nicolás's life and from that of his grandfather, Don Tino Veras, as well. Where once Tata, as Nicolás lovingly called him, had risen to tend to his little plot of land, its corn and beans, its sorghum and tomatoes; where once Nicolás helped Tata in the field when he could; where once the boy spent his weekdays in town, rooming at Ursula Granados's place so he could attend school, study the ABC's, learn the names of plants and animals, and consider the awesome importance of numbers; now chaos ruled their lives.

The school lay in ruins following a fierce battle between the army and the guerrillas of the FPL, the Popular Liberation Forces. Equally sorrowful, worship was no longer possible at the church. A year before, el padre Rugelio, a devotee of the Church's reform theology, had been accosted by a group of Guardia and beaten so severely his mind never was the same. Worse yet, there was this awful truth about the assault: to teach the queer communist a lesson, the Guardia bragged, a branch of jocote, thick as a wrist, had been thrust up his rectum. And so, with no priest to celebrate mass or even much of anything, with the church itself surrounded by suspicion and therefore steeped in danger, what else could the faithful do but stay away from it?

The morning gathered heat as the sun came fully up. It was the end of March and the height of summer. Only when the rains came in late May would the scorching heat of day be assuaged. The bus was not full—these days, given the situation, most buses traveling north into Chalatenango carried few people—and so it was easy to find a seat. Nicolás looked out the window and watched the countryside glide by: the brownness of parched earth; the dusty, motionless leaves of the trees; the scattered cattle and horses standing resignedly in the middle of withered pastures. Periodically, they passed a sugarcane field or a cornfield where the earth had been blackened by a recent burning, a deliberate act that prepared the soil for planting. The odor of seared earth caused a harsh inhalation. The farther north they climbed, the more the farmland gave way to rock strewn hills and gullies, deep ravines prickly with low-growing shrubbery interspersed with boulders outlined by foot trails and, in a few places, by ox cart paths. Dry creek beds rutted the bottoms of some ravines, and now and then, the meandering Lempa and then the Sumpul Rivers, their shallow waters brown with silt, showed themselves when the bus came around a bend. Struggling up the highway, the northbound bus groaned and lost speed as the driver shifted gears.

Nicolás leaned back against the seat and gave it a little

push, hoping to set it right, but it was useless. He felt sweat
dampen his shirt collar and drizzle down his sides. He
swiped his neck with a hand, and wiped his palm against the
tops of his thighs, covered by the thick denim of his blue
jeans. He opened his backpack and extracted a tortilla. On
his way to the bus terminal he had purchased a stack of
warm tortillas and a small brick of cheese. He broke off a
corner of cheese and ate it with his tortilla. He relished the
thought that he would surprise Tata with such extravagance.
Surprise him with his early presence, too, he was sad to say.
The plan had been for Nicolás to stay a while with his
mother in San Salvador, in the house of la niña Flor. What
Nicolás would say to Tata, coming home as he was, merely
a day after leaving, he had yet to decide: should he tell the
truth? That his mother was missing but that in all probability
she was safe at la niña Flor's? That he needed la niña Flor's
address to assure himself of it? Or should he simply spare
his grandfather any more distress than that which he daily
lived? Say to Tata, "I've come home for . . ." Come home
for what? To see to the spotted chicken? To Capitán, Tata's
rusty-colored dog? To Blanca, the white nanny goat?

Tata had bought the goat a few years back for the kids
she would have and the milk she would give that would
provide them extra income. Nicolás named her Blanca Nieves
because she was so white, and because at school the teacher
was reading a story about a lady, white as snow, who lived
in a cave with seven little men. The men had funny names,
and the children at school thought it amusing that one yawned
all the day, another sneezed so much, another laughed at
everything. Reyes Orellana, one of Nicolás's classmates,
asked the teacher why the little man who couldn't stop
sneezing didn't go to see a doctor. "Maybe he has allergies,"

Reyes explained. Carmelina, Reyes's mother, had allergies, and she had found pills to cure them at one of the people's health clinics over in El Carrizal. La señora Menjivar, the teacher, had stifled a grin and said she would look into it. Recalling his classmate made Nicolás sad. Reyes had been one of those who had died when guerrilleros took refuge in the school during a firefight and the army had riddled the place with their automatic weapons. The teacher had died, too. So had his friends Abel and Fidelina and Amado. Nicolás himself had been fortunate. He had been home that day with Tata, helping him pick corn.

Nicolás took another bite of tortilla. The sharp smell of the cheese aroused the old woman slumped against the window. She turned her head in Nicolás's direction and looked down at the tortilla and the cheese. Nicolás made a motion with his head that indicated he would share, and the old woman smiled a quick, toothless smile, which was her own way of accepting. She gummed the wedge of tortilla.

"Gracias, Chele," she said between chews.

"De nada," he replied.

She picked at a few crumbles of cheese that had fallen on her tapado, looking at him out of the corner of her eye. "You remind me of my grandson. He's slender like you. He's named Joaquín, after my son, though my son is dead now."

"Ah," Nicolás said, because it was clear she didn't so much want to converse as she wished to be heard.

She made a helpless gesture with a hand that communicated resignation. "Joaquín was a good man. A good father. Because he was an honest man, he enjoyed the respect of his neighbors. He was a man people could turn to when there was trouble and help was needed." She lifted her hand again and then let it drop into her lap. "Ay, but what good did it do him, all that honesty and helpfulness?" She fell into silence, and in respect Nicolás did likewise. He watched the countryside roll by.

After a moment, she resumed her story. She stared straight ahead as if peering into her past. "La Guardia killed him. In his own bed. At six o'clock in the morning. They came in and shot him in his bed."

Nicolás nodded, anxiety pricking at him. He thought about Alcides Naranjo, who had lived two doors down from Ursula Granados's house. It was said Alcides secretly belonged to UTC, the Fieldworkers' Union, an organization that fought for the rights of peasants and cooperatives. A year ago, someone from Orden, the paramilitary group ironically named Order, put the finger on him. Nicolás had been staying at Ursula's, and he heard the commotion up the street. Uniformed men marched up to Alcides's house. With the butts of their rifles, they banged on his door. They shouted, "This is the house of a communist!" before setting fire to the place. It flamed up like a stack of loose straw, Alcides Naranjo inside it. Now Nicolás was sitting next to the mother of someone the Guardia considered a subversive. He wanted to jump up and take another seat.

"But killing Joaquín in his own bed didn't satisfy them," the old woman went on. "Ah no. They had to cut off his head. La Guardia stuck my son's head on a post for the town to see. To teach them all a lesson, they said."

Nicolás could see she was about to say more, but the bus began to slow. He sat up straighter and looked down the aisle through the front window. "What's wrong?" the old woman asked. She grasped the seat in front and pulled herself up.

"Roadblock ahead," Nicolás replied.

"What's one more thing?" she said, dropping back upon the seat and clutching Nicolás's hand so quickly and so tightly he was taken aback. From his seat, he could see the line of rocks spanning the road, the soldiers with their rifles and camouflage gear standing purposefully across the pavement. With his free hand, Nicolás hastily shoved his backpack under the seat. He placed his feet flat on the floorboard in front of it. The flashlight was in the pack. Also the Swiss army knife with the folding tools. He was lucky that way. His mother worked for someone who frequently sent treats like this in his direction. More practical items, too. Items such as good clothing and sturdy boots. Out-of-the-ordinary things for a country boy like him to have.

The bus stopped with a loud hiss of brakes before the roadblock. The driver remained in his seat, all passengers in theirs. The driver pulled a crank and the bus door swung open with a squeaky sigh. One of the soldiers marched up the steps. He swept the interior of the bus with a glance, his M-16 rifle tucked under his arm and pointing at all of them. "ID," he said to the woman sitting in the first seat. When she handed over her card, he studied it carefully, comparing the photo on it to her face. He asked, "Where have you been? Where are you going? Where do you live?" Seemingly satisfied with both card and answers, he proceeded up the aisle.

A man sitting a few rows in front of Nicolás did not fare as well. Without even a glance at the ID he held up, the soldier barked "Out!" Nicolás watched the man go down the aisle. By slow degrees, the man's neck sank into his shoulders as he went. What happened next Nicolás could not observe, but he knew the routine just the same: another soldier on the road would make the man lift his arms and place them against the bus; with the barrel of his rifle he would spread the man's legs wide. A frisking would follow. The man would not be climbing on the bus again. Most certainly, it would be today's date that family and friends would give when telling the story of his disappearance.

"ID," the soldier said when he got to Nicolás's row. Because he was only nine, Nicolás did not possess identification papers, but the old woman did. She reached into the front of her tapado and extracted her papers. "He's my grandson. He's with me," she said to the soldier. She held on to Nicolás's hand with an iron-clad grip.

"Where are you going?" the soldier asked. He did not look up from the ID.

"Chalatenango," the old woman said. "We live there."

"Where have you been?"

"In Apopa. We went to see Clelia, my daughter. She's the boy's mother."

The soldier handed the ID back to the old woman. To Nicolás, he said, "And how is your mother?"

"My mother is fine," Nicolás said.

• • •

Nicolás got off the bus at Las Cañas. He boarded another going northeast to the town of Dulce Nombre de María, the largest town in the region. El Retorno, his village, was an hour's walk north. At the end of the main street (there were only two streets in the village: one going up and down, the other intersecting it), sat the little church constructed of adobe, so plain it did not possess a bell tower, much less a bell. On his way home, as his mother had taught him to do, Nicolás would stop and light a candle to la Virgen Milagrosa. Today he would do it in gratitude and thanks.

five

Where others not from El Retorno, mere passersby, would surely note the inherent harshness of its terrain and the dreariness the place educed, Nicolás saw something different. Where no color greeted the visitor's eye, but only the woeful tint of dust and soot, the indurate hue of stones pebbling the two intersecting streets, Nicolás saw a friendly palette of browns and duns and beiges. Because he had been born to this, because the view was his inheritance, it did not distress him. Nor did the sight of the buildings bordering the street. Humble houses and businesses shoring each other up and constructed of bahareque canes, mud packed in between and whitewashed in hopefulness. Over time, the walls of the buildings grew drab with grime, and soon the mud packing outlived its usefulness and chunks of it collapsed noiselessly into the street. The debris was never carted off; it remained there, to join the other evidence of how grim the times could be.

To Nicolás this was home, and in its simple direness he recognized his life and what he had lived and what he had yet to live, and because it belonged to him, he accepted it. This he felt deep inside himself, and were he asked to explain it, he would have to shrug and maybe say he did not understand the question.

Returning to El Retorno only a day after leaving, with his absence so fresh that memory had no chance to add or detract from it, Nicolás stood in the middle of his village street and saw it was deserted. The mid-afternoon heat, dull and intense, pressed down on him, and there was a sort of powdery stink in the air he did not recognize. He pulled his shirttail out of his jeans and used it to mop his face. He hiked up his backpack, feeling the odd nudge of his mother's shoe against his back. He stepped to the side of the street and under the wide tile overhang of Doña Paulina's store. Its doors were shut tight, something rare as March rain, especially during these times when los muchachos, the guerrillas, hiding in the hills a short hike away, could pop up at any time, when the army could swoop in after them, in the end both sides proving to be ready customers. Though a war raged and cash was scarce, the times did not mitigate the need for sugar and cornmeal, cooking oil and lard, salt and coffee. Not surprisingly, the situation intensified the demand for batteries, matches, and cigarettes.

Nicolás stepped slowly down the street as heat rose from it and from the snarled tangle of brush forming its background. The drone of cicadas descended from the trees. He passed Ursula Granados's tortilla-making place. Her door was not closed. Nicolás looked in on the familiar galvanized tubs filled to overflowing with corn dough, on the two beehive ovens with the huge clay griddles on top. It was on these wide pottery rounds that tortillas were cooked, but today the ovens beneath them were cold, for no firewood glowed in the side openings. At a time when the shop should have been bustling, Ursula was absent.

Nicolás went inside. The store had one large room with a back door that opened up to a patio and to Ursula's living quarters. He pinched a bit of masa from one of the tubs, noting the crustiness of the dough's top layer. He poked a finger deep into the mound and felt the moistness there. Five browned tortillas were fanned out on a comal like a hand of cards. Nicolás gathered up the tortillas, noting how hard and brittle they were. He stepped to the back door and opened it, calling out across the treeless patio: "Are you there, Niña Ursula? It's me, Nico Veras." He used the word niña, to address the owner; it meant "girl," and it was used as a term of endearment for women of all ages. He had crossed this patio countless times, had slept curled like a baby on a straw mat spread under the roof of the narrow gallery that fronted Ursula's room.

No answer came to his first hello, so he called a second time. Still no reply. He recrossed the room and stepped back onto the street. He was very alert now. He moved cautiously toward the church, fear pricking at the nape of his neck. He looked down and realized that he had come away with the tortillas. He gave a quick laugh, more to calm himself than because he thought it funny. When he got home, he would feed the tortillas to the goat and the hen. He continued up the street, passing the village's excuse for a pharmacy, and saw that its door, too, was shut. He shifted his eyes keenly from side to side, straining to detect any movement. He breathed lightly, the better to hear. He wished for wings with which to fly home to his grandfather.

Where the main street intersected with the second, Nicolás turned the corner. What he saw caused him to drop the tortillas. Where once there had been a street lined with houses and businesses, the school even—though it had been in shambles for months—there was now a crazy disarray of broken buildings and rubble. Don Pablo's house was half gone. La niña Delfina's as well. The house of Doña Orbelina and her daughter María Clara had totally collapsed. On the corner, where once stood the garage of Emilio Sánchez, the auto mechanic, now nothing remained but gaping walls and a short span of roof. In the midst of this, gray-black smoke rose up from the smoldering wreckage.

Beholding such devastation, Nicolás's apprehension turned into full-blown fear. He looked beyond the street and its jumble of ruins, beyond the trees and over the hills toward the place where his home stood, a two-hour walk away. He thought: Tata, are you there?

Nicolás picked up the stiff tortillas and stuffed them into his backpack. He sidestepped down the street, avoiding the debris that littered it: the chunks of shattered walls, the brick-red shards that had once been tile roofs, the unrecognizable detritus that just yesterday had been a family's possessions. When he got to Emilio Sánchez's repair shop, or what remained of it, Emilio was poking with a stick at a mound of smoking rubbish as if searching for something of great value.

Out of habit, Nicolás stepped through what once had been the entrance to the shop, but where now only a door frame stood with but stubby triangles of wall attached to it. "Don Emilio!" Nicolás exclaimed. "What happened?"

Emilio Sánchez looked up from the rubble; he wore no shirt, only trousers and shoes. He had tied a kerchief around his neck, and the cloth was stiff with grime. The ribs in his bared chest were as pronounced as the ribs of the dog that stood patiently close by with its tail curled under him like a long, inverted C. Piled around the two were chunks of adobe and lengths of bahareque, and what remained of the work-table, the benches, the shelving, the myriad cans the shelving had held, cans containing nails and gaskets and screws, coils of wire, pieces of pipe and tubing, all the many things that are part and parcel of the mechanic's trade.

"The army bombed us," Emilio said, as casually as if he were speaking of the weather. "Sons of a bitch guerrilleros. Until they came on the scene, and the unions and coopera-tives, we had a peaceful little town. Now it's nothing but security forces and fights with guerrillas. Now this." He shook his head ruefully. "As if bombs weren't enough, my acetylene tank blew up."

"What about the hills?" Nicolás asked. "Did they bomb in the hills?" He pointed toward home, drawing in a breath against Emilio's answer.

Emilio stopped poking in the rubble. "Weren't you up there?" he said. "Didn't you just come down from there?"

"No. I was in San Salvador with my mother."

To show his understanding, Emilio Sánchez lifted his chin a fraction. "I think the hills are safe," he said. "The sons of bitches were aiming for the guerrilleros who have been hiding, over there, by the river. When the bombing be-gan, it rousted them from their holes. A bunch of them came running through town and the planes followed. I was in Pau-lina's store when we heard the roar of them coming."

As Emilio spoke, Nicolás allowed himself a tiny wedge of relief, but only that. "When did this happen?"

"Yesterday. In the early morning."

"I left at dawn."

"Well, you were lucky, boy. You missed this newest little gift the army bestowed on us." Emilio gave a snort that was meant to be a laugh. "Bomber planes did this. They launched rockets, too." Emilio snorted a second time. "The army's trying out the gringos' latest gift. Leftover planes from Vietnam."

"Where is everybody?"

"Everybody took off. Everybody but me." Emilio pointed away with his stick, then he went back to digging in the smoky rubble. "Except, of course, for those who fell in the bombing."

"Who fell?" Since the war began, that verb had become a common euphemism for loss of life.

Emilio Sánchez used his free hand to gesture vaguely up the street. "Doña Orbelina. La María Clara. Their house was blown up. We had to dig them out."

"¿Y don Pablo? ¿Y la Delfina?"

"They were hurt, but not bad enough they couldn't leave."

"¿Y la niña Ursula? I was just in her place."

"She left with Paulina." Emilio hunched his shoulders. "No, Nico. Everybody left. Even the guerrilleros took to higher ground. They left their dead and hauled off their wounded."

"Just one day I was gone, and all this happened."

"You should have stayed away longer."

Nicolás nodded. "I'm going home. You come, too. You can stay with me and Tata. We have a place we can hide in for when we are pressed." He would not be too specific. Sometimes, Tata said, even your friends can turn out to be the enemy.

Emilio Sánchez snorted again. "Thanks, but no. I'm staying for the moment at the church. They got the church, too, by the way."

"The church?"

"The sons of bitches ruined half of it."

• • •

Nicolás looked up the hill. The ground alongside the church and sloping down toward him was a series of wounds. The exposed rocky earth showed how thin the topsoil truly was. Most of the church's roof was gone, and the sunlight pointed out the damage. The conacaste that for all of Nicolás's life had shaded the building still stood, but its massive trunk was ripped down the middle and showed the long slash of its heart, a tender pale yellow. Half the tree had been brought down, and the branches and leaves had fallen into the church.

Nicolás climbed the hill, his fear renewing itself. Was there anything in his life that the war could not touch? He stepped over the remnants of the east wall and the jumble of desecration: half the main altar had been shattered. The other half was pinned and hidden behind the downed branches of conacaste. The pews lay broken and skewed, one section at cross-purposes with another. Sections of wall and roof and windows lay like teeter-totter planks across these. The west wall appeared to be intact, but that side of the church lay in shadows. It was this wall that contained the niche in which reposed the statue of la Virgen Milagrosa. Nicolás picked his way carefully over the wreckage toward her; as he went he dispersed the dust motes the sunny air sent up around him.

He found the niche intact, the milagros—little tin cutouts in the form of cows, goats, pigs and oxen, ears of corn and bean pearls, various parts of the body such as eyes, legs, hands, and hearts—that people had nailed there in thanks for miracles granted still tacked like chain mail around the niche's opening. But the space itself was empty. Nicolás fingered his own Milagrosa medal hanging from the chain

around his neck and began his search. He squatted and
slowly duck-walked among the dark debris, crunching
shards of votive glass under his boot heels. He squinted
through the pale, dusty light, groping blindly for la Virgen.
Then he remembered his flashlight and opened his backpack.
The odor of tortillas, both fresh and stale, and of the hunk
of cheese he had purchased just that morning, wafted up
when he dug inside. He pulled out the flashlight and resumed
his search with brighter prospects for success.

He found her tucked beneath a section of splintered pew.
He pulled the statue out from under, then put his flashlight
away. He inspected her in the sun, using his shirttail to wipe
her clean. She was two hand spans tall, fashioned from pine
washed over with blue and white paint; with gold and silver
paint, too. The craftsman who had carved her had used one
solid piece of wood to form the body, robe, and veil. Our
Lady's arms, crooked slightly at the elbows, and the little
crown atop her head had each been tooled from separate
pieces. Nicolás noted that an edge of Our Lady's gilded
crown was broken off and that her left arm had snapped off
at the elbow. The light beams the hand had projected—three
strips of pointed wood painted silver—were missing, but he
could see them as clearly as if they were there. The right arm
was intact, and so was the hand, palm up and small as a
seashell, but the light beams from this hand also were gone.
A deep gash formed a rent on the back of the cloak; another,
like a tiny teardrop, marred the cheek under one eye. Nicolás
stared into la Virgen's china-blue eyes. "You're safe with
me," he said to her. He would take her home, and she herself
would make things right there. He gave the statue one more
swipe with his shirttail and eased it into the side of his backpack. He found that she just fit, resting securely against the
little boat that was his mother's shoe.

six

The trip from El Retorno was never easy. The route jogged up and down rocky hills and jagged ravines. Creeks snaked along the bottom of some canyons, but in the dry season the arroyos could be spanned in three wide steps or four. Vegetation choked the gullies, some of its varieties, more than inhospitable, were downright menacing: in the low spots, dense bamboo stands with their fuzzy sharp leaves, the fiery chichicaste shrubs, the pointed spines of the izote. Along the ridge tops, scraggly pine and cypress grew like the stiff short hairs on the backs of riled hogs. Cassia and morro and jocote thrived God-knew-how in the impoverished soil. Amid it all sprouted the nondescript flora that was neither shrub nor tree, only a sorry excuse for something green and growing.

In the rainy season, all was transformed. The blessed moisture plumped the foliage and cleansed the leaves of the choking dust that for months had smothered them. In the creeks, the water rose high and ran so swiftly as to cause maddening detours. When it rained, boulders, rocks, stones, and pebbles used the wetness to show off hidden qualities: their striking veins, the deep rich colors, the patterns pointing to the phases of evolution that over time each object had endured. Still, in wet season or dry, a rock, a stone, or even a pebble could trip a traveler. Send a traveler tumbling down some steep barranco.

Making the trip today, Nicolás avoided such missteps. His boots made the going easier. They had high, fawn-colored tops and thick rubber soles; metal hooks held the leather laces. His mother had brought them home a year ago, one of the best gifts la niña Flor had ever provided. Nicolás had been sitting on the bench under a copinol honing the blade of his machete with a pumice stone when Capitán's barks announced his mother's approach. Nicolás watched her striding determinedly down the path under the archway trees that led to the rancho. The dog rushed to meet her, his fierce yelps betrayed by a wagging tail. His mother had slung the tied-together laces over her shoulder, and the front boot bumped against her chest as she walked. "Look what I brought you," she said when she reached him. Capitán's fuss had roused Tata, who had been resting in his hammock in the hut. He came out as Nicolás was trying on the boots. They all held their breaths against their being too small. As it happened, they were a bit large, a much better develop-ment.

This afternoon, Nicolás did not stop to rest, although his shirt was soaked with sweat from his exertion. At every bend he expected a retreating guerrillero to step from behind a ledge, or a frightened town person to materialize on a path. Our Lady was at his back, and she was like a firm hand driving him up the hills, easing the fear blossoming inside him, the fear that what he would find at home would be like what he had left behind. He dug his chin into his chest and trudged toward the ridge, now just minutes away, which widened eventually into the tract of land that encompassed his home. When at last he topped the ridge, he spied the line of trees—marañon, copinol, mango, and zapote—that canopied the rancho. They were second-growth trees, spindly and middle-sized, but they looked glorious because they were upright and undisturbed. The enchanted song of the cicadas welcomed him. Keeping under the shade of the trees, Nicolás followed the well-tended path that led to his door. He gave a whoop at the sight of the two little rooms topped with palm fronds, the cooking shed and its red-tiled roof nestled up beside them. In all the world, was there a lovelier sight? He was steps from home when he stopped in his tracks. Capitán. Where was the dog? Why had he not barked?

"Tata!" Nicolás shouted. "Tata, are you there?"

Silence.

Nicolás trotted into the main room of the rancho. It was empty, but everything in it appeared normal. The hammocks, unhooked at one end, hung down the wall and formed mesh puddles upon the hardened earth floor. The dresser stood against another wall, lopsided as it always had been. Above it were tacked three religious pictures in varying sizes: one of Our Lady, another of Jesús, the third of San Jude, Saint of the Impossible. In the second room, the table and three chairs, once painted a bright green and now peeling in spots down to bare wood, sat in their customary places. In the kitchen shed, the fire ring outlined by four big stones entrenched in the floor had only cold ash heaped inside it.

Nicolás went outside and sat on the bench in the yard. Nearby, the speckled hen was roosting on a low branch of a zapote. She gave a little cluck at the company, then buried her neck back into her feathers. All is normal, Nicolás thought, and felt calmer, although Tata's absence still unsettled him. Then it came to him, a thought so logical he felt foolish for not thinking it before: Tata was fishing. He was at the river. Nicolás jumped up and ran back into the rancho. Tata's fishing net was not piled upon one of the chairs in the second room, its usual place. The turquoise bucket he used to bring his catch home was also gone. Thank you, Virgencita, he said to her from inside his head. He sat back down under the trees and unhooked the backpack from his shoulders and carefully placed it beside him. Most probably Tata had gone downstream, to that lucky spot on the Sumpul that was close to town and where he always found fish. This time, with the sun moving down, was a good time for catching tilapia. So was early morning, when the mist was just beginning to rise off the water.

Nicolás hauled himself up because an image of the nanny goat popped suddenly into his head. When Tata went fishing, he always chained Blanca up in the cave lest she attempt to trot after him. Nicolás pulled the flashlight from his backpack and fetched his machete from the kitchen shed, then headed for the cave.

The cave was a hollow inside a small hill that rose behind the hut. Nicolás himself had discovered it two years before, after a huge boulder had rolled down an opposing hill during an afternoon thunderstorm. Nicolás and his grandfather had felt the ground tremble under them as the big stone roared down. When the storm passed and the sun shone anew, Nicolás emerged to investigate the impact of the weather. As he traced the track of the marauding boulder, he discovered that as it tumbled it had crushed all vegetation in its path, including the sturdy vines and tangled foliage that through time had concealed the cave's opening.

The cavern was not large. The interior could be stepped

off in five broad paces in one direction, six in the other. There was enough headroom for even Tata to stand up comfortably. Nature itself had carved ledges into the walls, so that when candles were set out the cave resembled a chapel. As if this newfound sanctuary were not good fortune enough, another section jutted off from the first, forming a steep, low-ceilinged tunnel that burrowed down into the earth and opened up a few meters from the riverbank. These discoveries were made during the wet season, when the river was high and the tunnel half filled with water, and where it led could not then be discerned. But when the rains ended and the river dropped, the tunnel dried out. With stooped heads they could walk down it right to the Sumpul.

The two had worked off and on for weeks to make the cave serviceable. Their labor was difficult, because the boulder rolled up at the entrance had nearly resealed it. To get in, they had to drop down on their knees and wiggle past one of the narrow slits that remained between the rock edge and the cave mouth. They used their hoes and machetes, implements slim enough to fit through the opening, to dig up rocks and stones embedded in the cave floor, to make the floor level and round the wall ledges. Air flowed in around the rock. Light, more or less bright, depending on the position of the sun, leaked in through the same places. Still, the cave was stuffy, and when half the tunnel was filled with water the walls were damp and furry with moss.

Later, when the weather changed and the tunnel dried out, they stocked their secret sanctuary with supplies of corn and beans, salt, sugar, coffee and cornmeal, candles and matches. They carried in a pottery jug for storing water. To improve the ventilation, Tata chopped bamboo from the bottoms of ravines and dragged it home. With great effort, he twisted hollow lengths of bamboo through the narrowest side of the cave and out into the hillside. Two extra hammocks were brought in and hung from hooks driven into rock. By day, the folded hammocks hung limp against the cave wall. At night, they stretched open wall to wall to keep Tata and Nicolás off the floor and away from insects and lizards.

Now, Nicolás approached the cave in the customary roundabout way, for what good was a secret cave if a tramped-down path could point to it. When he reached the entrance, he leaned around the big stone and turned on the flashlight. With the edge of the machete, he drew aside the trumpet vines obscuring the narrow opening. He wormed his way in, shining the light ahead of him. "Blanca," he said, for as he entered she was there waiting, bleating a hello.

seven

Nicolás and the goat emerged from the tunnel's river exit. Nicolás scanned the bank of the stream for Tata, but there was no sign of him. While the thirsty Blanca drank her fill, Nicolás climbed the hill and collected his backpack. From it, he took one of the stale tortillas and offered it to the goat. As she fell upon it with gusto, Nicolás took out la Virgen and lowered her into the warm river water. He rubbed her gently with his thumb, careful not to cause her further harm. When the statue was as clean as he could get it, he stashed her in the backpack again.

The feel of water made Nicolás realize how sweaty and grimy he was, so he unhooked the laces of his boots and slipped out of them, and his clothes as well. He waded into the river, using the flat stones just under the surface as a path to deeper water. Soon he was up to his waist, as high as the river would rise at this time of year. He flattened himself out and floated, allowing the lazy current to cradle him. Lulled by the sound of the cicadas, he watched the hills and the trees around him change color as the sun disappeared behind the ridge. In the muting light, the surroundings looked almost beautiful, the hillsides sleek and green with growth, the sky above a splash of indigo. The river was beautiful, too; its water smooth and lead colored, its pebbled banks a deeper hue than river water.

Nicolás loved the Sumpul. In school, la señora Menjivar (may she rest in peace) pointed out the river on a map to show how long and significant it was. In some places, she said, the Sumpul formed the border between El Salvador and Honduras. "That's an important job," she added, laying a finger on the map on this spot and then on that. The fact did not impress Nicolás, for it was an abstract concept, and as such it did not touch him. What did was the Sumpul itself, meandering just a short hike down the hill from his home. The Sumpul provided water to drink and water in which to bathe. The Sumpul offered up its fish. The Sumpul was Nicolás's own personal river, yet though he loved it, there were times when he feared it. At dusk, when it was bad luck to cross it. And in the deep of night. After the thousands of frogs raised their myriad voices, that was when the Ziguanaba could appear. La Ziguanaba, the madwoman of legend with the savage-looking eyes and the long, wild hair. La Ziguanaba, who had abandoned her small son and who, because of it, was sentenced to roam the riverbanks in search of him. Sometimes, as Nicolás lay in his hammock, he could hear the agonizing wails of the woman even above the cacophony of the frogs. More than anything else he feared the incontrovertible truth: were he to somehow find himself at the riverbank when la Ziguanaba passed by, he would be powerless against her manic laughter, against her lures. Nothing he might do could keep him from the flailing arms that would snatch him up. In a blink of an eye, and before he could escape, she would turn him into a deranged old woman like herself.

His mother always tried to calm his fears about such things. At the thought of her, tears burned at the rims of Nicolás's eyes. Before he could stop himself, he let out a sob. Mamá, he said, but he only mouthed the word. He pinched his nose and dunked his head into the river, washing both tears and sobs away, coming up again in a great burst of flying water. On the bank, the goat was going after his bootlaces, so Nicolás strode out of the water and shook himself dry as Capitán always did. He shooed the goat away and she responded with a reproving bleat. He pulled his clothes back on, wrestling into his jeans. He dried each foot with an opposite hand, slipped into his socks and boots again. "Come, Blanca," he said. "Let's get you some fodder."

• • •

It was dark now, and Nicolás busied himself in the kitchen shed. He had started a fire under the grate and the griddle that spanned the cornerstones of the fire ring. He rewarmed the coffee left in the pot and placed the tortillas he had bought that morning directly on the burning coals. When they were hot, he gobbled them up. He ate the wedge of cheese as well, washing it down with a long drink of coffee. Though he had milked Blanca and whitened the coffee and added a palmful of sugar as well, the brew remained bitter, and he had to spit out the grounds.

The fire he had made was the only source of illumination, and the flames flickered as he reflected on Tata and where he might be. He thought about his mother and what he should do to find her again. He now knew her employers' proper name and where the family lived. He had dug in the dresser and taken out the box containing a few of his treasures and his mother's letters. In it, he had also found the pad of paper, the envelopes, and the stamps she had bought for

him to write her back. To get him started, she had addressed
one of the envelopes to herself: "Leticia María Veras, a cargo
de Sra. Florencia de Salah, Altos Colónia Escalón, San Salvador." She had placed a ten-centavo stamp on the corner.
The stamp bore the image of José Matías Delgado, a found-
ing father of the country. Nicolás bit the inside of his lip,
chastising himself for having never used the envelope, feeling
guilty at the thought of his mother waiting each day for it
to arrive.

Nicolás stood and steeled himself for what he had to do:
he would take his things and the goat and go to the cave.
With Tata away, it would be a safer place in which to pass
the night. To get there, he would have to walk down the
path to the river. He prayed la Ziguanaba was resting tonight.

• • •

Nicolás shined the flashlight around the interior of the cave.
Blanca had trotted ahead. She was already inside, her neck
outstretched and begging for the bag of corn stored on one
of the wall ledges. Nicolás had lugged in a bucket filled with
water. He set it down, placed the flashlight on its end, groped
for the matches, and lighted a tall candle. Its light softened
the odd contours of the cave, transforming the space into a
grotto blessed with the odor of exposed earth and deep en-
closure. Nicolás turned off the flashlight because, thanks to
Tata's admonishments, he was careful to conserve batteries,
which were expensive and difficult to obtain. Nicolás poured
corn onto the ground, giving Blanca an extra treat to distract
her while he chained her up.

Because she had brought him safely down the dark path
and along the river's edge, la Virgen Milagrosa needed spe-

cial attention. Nicolás set her on the ledge nearest the entrance stone; it was the smallest of the ledges and looked much like a niche. Same as church, he thought, and he moved her around until he was certain she could not topple. He carried the candle over, the light glimmering in his cupped hands, and set it beside her.

He stretched his hammock across the cave and hooked it up, then picked up his machete and laid it next to the hammock. He collapsed into his bed. Serenaded by the madrigal created by the frogs, he drifted off to sleep.

• • •

Sometime in the night, Nicolás woke up to a voice. Shaking the sleep from his head, he reached for his machete. He laid the hilt against his chest, the end of it over the hammock's side.

In the stillness, and over the racing of his heart, the voice came again: "Nicolás, no tengás miedo. Fear not, Nicolás."

He lifted his head and looked in the direction of the niche. Rays of light, slender as moonbeams, projected from la Virgen's right hand, from the place where her left hand used to be. He heard the voice again: "Fear not, Nicolás, I am your mother, too, and I am with you." After a short time, the light from Our Lady's hands grew dim and disappeared. Only the light of the candle remained.

Nicolás waited expectantly, head up and straining to hear, but the small, calm voice did not come again.

eight

Nicolás rubbed sleep from his eyes and rolled clumsily from the hammock. Morning haloed around the entrance rock; the candle had burned down to a dim nub. Daylight disclosed that Tata had not returned. To calm himself, Nicolás created reasons why this might be: Tata wasn't expecting him. Tata stopped to spend the night with a neighbor. He had gone farther downriver than usual. Nicolás told himself these things, but the truth was that in all the years he had lived at the rancho, Tata had never failed to come home after evening fishing.

Nicolás turned to la Virgen, reposing in the niche. She had spoken to him last night. "Do not be afraid," she had said in a quiet voice. Sleek beams of light had issued from her tiny hands, from the one she still had and the phantom one she had lost. He had seen that light, had he not?

Blanca was pulling at her chain, making a racket and trying to reach the bag of corn. He unchained her, scooped out a few handfuls of grain, and heaped them on the ground. He piled a smaller amount next to Our Lady. In case you're hungry, he said to her, but in his head. He listened for her response, but none came, and he felt foolish for believing she

45

could speak. Her damaged arm was only what it was: a formed piece of wood severed at the elbow. The other arm, though whole, was but the shape of an arm and an opened palm, nothing more. From neither place did light beams shine. Clearly he had dreamed it all: the light, the voice— yet there was no less comfort in the fact. While he slept, she had instructed him, and he would heed her advice and not be afraid.

The box containing his mother's letters was still where he had placed it last night. It reminded him of what he must do. He must leave the rancho at once and pursue his plan to find her. He opened the box and poked one of her letters into his backpack. He stashed the box on end in the niche beside his statue. Traveling back to San Salvador, she would light the path that would return him to his mother.

Nicolás heard a scuttling sound and turned to see the goat rounding the corner that led down the tunnel. All her corn was gone, and now she was off to the river for a drink. Nicolás chided himself for unchaining her. Now he would have to fetch her and bring her back before he could start for the capital.

• • •

The goat was not at the river. When Nicolás emerged from the tunnel, he jogged along the riverbank and caught sight of her scrambling up the hill path toward home. He broke into a run, grumbling his displeasure as he went. When he crested the hill, he saw what it was that had drawn her.

There were strangers in the yard. They had rifles. They were dressed in the ragtag uniform of the people's army, the FPL.

nine

Nicolás bolted down the hill. Halfway to the river, he lost his footing and began sliding on his rump along the path. It was strewn with pebbles and, try as he might to slow himself, his momentum carried him bumping down almost to the water's edge.

Small trees and shrubs lined the path, and he prayed they had concealed him; that his descent, though rapid, was quiet enough to remain undetected; that he could scurry back into the cave again. This would have been so were it not for the guerrillero who stepped out of the brush on a slant of ground a few paces from the river. The man had a rifle hanging from his shoulder and he was pulling up his zipper. When he saw Nicolás, he gave a little start and then instantly composed himself.

"Where you going, boy?" the guerrillero said. He was not old. Maybe in his twenties. He wore a tattersall shirt, its tails hanging over his trousers. A worn khaki hat with a wide circular brim covered his head.

"I fell," Nicolás said, remaining as he was. His hands were raw and stinging from the downward slide.

"You were in a big hurry."

"I tripped."

"Who are you?"

"I live here," Nicolás said. He stood up slowly, keeping his arms up and away from himself as Tata had taught him to do.

"Well, if you live here, you better try the climb again. This time, step carefully as you go." The guerrillero pointed at the ground with his rifle.

Nicolás proceeded cautiously up the hill, not so much to heed the advice but because he needed a minute or two to think. He yearned for the feel of the machete in his hand—if for nothing else for the reassurance it provided—but he had left the knife in the cave, a place he could not allow strangers to discover.

Capitán rounded the corner of the rancho as Nicolás stepped into the yard. The mutt gave a bark of recognition and trotted over. For a moment, the dog's presence disconcerted Nicolás, but then understanding struck and he yelled, "Tata!" and ran toward the house.

His grandfather was slumped on the bench under the copinol. At Nicolás's cry, he jumped up and came rushing to his grandson. They fell into each other's arms. Nicolas felt the warm bulk of Tata's chest against his cheek but could not speak. Only sobs escaped his lips, and he did not have the strength to hold them back. He let the tears run, and, after a time, he took in a long shuddering breath, feeling the comfort of Tata's big hand upon the crown of his head. "Vaya, vaya, vaya," Tata soothed, his words keeping rhythm with the pats of his hand.

Nicolás wiped away his tears. He was with Tata now. Tata with the long rutted face the color of tamarind. Tata with his faded blue shirt as soft as an old sheet. Tata with

his spindly legs poking out of the baggy trousers he had
rolled up to the knees, a fastidious habit he repeated frequently throughout the day. Tata with his brown callused
feet shod in wide sandals carved from rubber tires. Nicolás
bent to scratch Capitán behind the ears. The dog's tail was
a blurred whip; he gave little grunts of satisfaction.

"Come," Tata said. He repositioned his straw hat upon
his head and led Nicolás back to the bench. The guerrillero
in the tattersall shirt had posted himself at the entrance to
the cooking shed. Another guerrillero, this one sporting a
thick mustache, was at the rancho door. A lighted cigarette
dangled from his lips. He had a rifle at his side. Both men
kept their eyes upon the two on the bench.

"Who are they?" Nicolás whispered. They were not
formidable-looking men, although any man in possession of
a rifle was formidable enough.

Tata asked a question of his own: "What are you doing
here? You're supposed to be with your mother."

The suddenness of the question befuddled Nicolás, and
he answered it with another one: "Tata, what happened to
you last night?"

Before Tata could say anything, a stout imposing woman
emerged from the cooking shed. She reminded Nicolás of
someone, and then he realized that, in size, she looked like
the owner of the place where he had eaten in San Salvador.
But this woman was much younger. She was dressed in
worn-out jeans with thick socks turned down over laced-up
boots. An awesome belt cinched her waist. An M-16 rifle
was strapped casually over one shoulder. The woman sauntered over. "I'm Dolóres," she said. "And what do we call
you?" She held out a hand to Nicolás.

"He's my grandson," Tata said. "He's a good boy,

though I'm wondering what he's doing here. A few days ago, I sent him off with his mother to San Salvador."

"Nicolás. My name is Nicolás Veras." He took Dolóres's hand.

"I didn't think you'd be back," Tata said, his mind obviously locked on the subject. "Why did you come back?"

Nicolás paused for a moment before answering. He did not wish to launch into the puzzling truth about his mother; not just now, he did not. Instead, he said the first thing that popped into his head. "We heard El Retorno had been bombed. I had to come back. I had to make sure you were all right."

"The army," Dolóres said, shaking her head. "Can you believe them? Picking on a place like El Retorno?" She gave a grunt of disgust, then added, "So, Nicolás Veras, I'll now tell you what I told your grandfather earlier. We are all thankful for your hospitality."

Nicolás looked quickly at Tata for some sort of confirmation.

"She's the boss," Tata said.

"The boss?" Nicolás replied.

"That's right. She's the captain," Tata said. "She's the one in charge."

ten

Dolóres squatted down, the denim of her jeans stretched tight over her thick thighs. Her M-16 rested like a bridge between them. "You need to know a few things," she said to Nicolás. The fact that she addressed him was confounding, and he glanced at Tata, hoping to catch an explanation from his eyes. But Tata's countenance betrayed no inner feelings. Nicolás took Tata's stolidness as a signal, and set his own face into a mask.

Dolóres spoke in a measured, assured voice, like the schoolteacher used to do, Nicolás thought. "We are part of the Popular Liberation Forces. We are the people's army and as such we are an army comprised of the poor. At present, with revolution in its infancy, we are small, but daily we grow in number. We wage battles here in the mountains of Chalatenango, as well as to the east of us, in the department of Morazán. We battle to eradicate poverty and ignorance and ill health. We battle to defend ourselves against the National Army, the Guardia, against Orden and other repressive forces. For now, we work in small groups, but more and more the people join us to fight the great fight. I tell you this so you will know that we are strong. That we are much more than the three of us you see here. There are many of us fighting the fight of the people."

"Not me," Tata interrupted. "I live up here on the mountain under my trees. Nicolás and I, we keep to ourselves. We make no trouble."

"But you're in trouble all the same," Dolóres replied.

"And how is that? We've done nothing. We are simple country people."

Nicolás heard his grandfather's words, and he was proud he had been included in the statement. They were partners, he and Tata. Together, through everything.

With an outstretched hand, Dolóres indicated the rancho and the surrounding area. "This place is yours, but it won't be yours for long. Without us to prevent it, one day the enemy will come and seize it. The enemy will cut down your trees. He will take over your cornfield, your bean field, that little square of land down by the river where your sorghum likes to grow. The enemy will burn your crops, when and if you get crops planted. The enemy will roast your goat." She pointed to Blanca, who was nibbling a volunteer shrub that had rooted under a zapote. "The enemy likes goat, you know. It likes beef. It likes chicken, too." Dolóres leaned in a little as if to make a finer point. "Look how close they've come already. A few days ago, they bombed El Retorno. That will satisfy them for a time, especially now that the bombing drove us from our place of entrenchment. But make no mistake, they'll be looking for us soon enough."

Over by the shed entrance, the man in the tattersall shirt nodded in agreement.

Nicolás listened, his mind churning at the thought of Blanca turning on a spit.

"If you hide out here," Tata said, "you will bring the army to our mountain."

"They would come anyway. And we must prepare ourselves for that day. In this changing reality," Dolóres said, "we do what we must. A few of us must sacrifice for the good of the rest."

"You're going to hide here?" Nicolás asked, the impact of Dolóres's words finally dawning on him.

She nodded. "You're in the ideal spot. Up the mountain, out of the way, and under the trees. Your place is difficult to get to, easy to defend. More of my people are on the way."

"How many?" Tata asked.

"There should be about twenty of us. My unit and the one of a compañero who fell during the bombing at El Retorno. The first of the bunch will arrive by noon. They'll be coming with supplies and provisions."

"Who told you about us?" Nicolás said.

"That, Nicolás Veras, is not for you to worry about. There are many who happily provide us with information. It's their contribution to the cause."

"What do you want with us?" Tata asked.

"As I've said to you before, we want your hospitality. For the duration of our stay, that's what we want."

Tata set his face. "And what if we deny it? This hospitality you seek?"

Dolóres gave a little laugh. "Well, naturally, we'd prefer that you extended it. But whether you give it or not, we are a determined bunch. You can leave, of course. We won't hold you back."

"I'd never leave my rancho," Tata said.

"A fine decision on your part, Don Tino. Others might take the chance and head down the hill to seek out the army and tell them we are here. But you know the army, don't you, Don Tino? As far as the army is concerned, the mere fact we are here, occupying your little rancho, turns you into sympathizers, does it not?"

Tata was silent for a moment, then he said, "And how long do you plan to stay?"

Dolóres looked off across the yard and shrugged. "Not long, but as long as it takes. Or until the enemy drives us out." She turned her face toward Tata's again. "Until then, we need time to regroup. To strategize. After the bombing, we have a few wounded. They need care and rest. We'll set up a treatment area so we can tend to them." Dolóres stood. She slung her rifle strap over a shoulder again. "We'll need to build lean-tos. Your rooms over there"—she jutted her chin in the direction of the rancho—"we'll use one for surgery when surgery is needed."

Tata rose to meet Dolóres eye to eye. "You can't do surgery here."

"And why not?" she asked.

"It's not right to do it here. The floors are dirt; there are insects and vermin . . ."

"Believe me, Don Tino," Dolóres said, "we've operated on people in worse places than this." She went on, "Like I said, we'll build lean-tos. We'll build beds so we can get the wounded up off the ground. We need bamboo for all that. I see you have bamboo, Don Tino. I saw it piled out back."

Now it was Tata's turn to nod.

"We'll be using it. We'll be using your kitchen shed, too. Carmen, our cook, is on the way. Before you know it, you'll have a field kitchen here. Tortillas, rice, and beans. You don't mind that, do you? Coffee, too. And don't you worry. We won't be roasting your nanny goat. We'll use her for milk."

"She's a good milker," Nicolás said.

"I'm glad to hear it. That's what this army of ours needs, good producers. Good workers. I'm sure you're a good worker, Nicolás Veras," Dolóres said. "You look strong and you have good shoes. Good shoes are important to the work we do." She lifted one foot and then the other, showing off her own good boots.

"Are you taking my boots?" Nicolás asked, alarmed. "They're a gift from my mother."

Dolóres threw her head back and gave a hearty laugh. "You can keep your shoes, Nicolás Veras. Those shoes will come in handy for the work you have ahead." She motioned to her muchachos. "Okay, boys, let's take a look at that bamboo."

• • •

When only Tata and Nicolás were left under the copinol, Tata sat on the bench again.

"What are we going to do?" Nicolás asked. He wanted to add that he was hungry. It was maybe eight o'clock, and he'd had not even a drink of water.

Tata shook his head. "We have to bide our time. Wait for the others to show up and see what's in store."

"She said they're putting me to work."

"They'll put both of us to work, no question about that."

"What do you think they'll make us do?" Nicolás imagined a bandanna triangling the bottom half of his face. He imagined a rifle being thrust into his hands, his having to burst into a place like the school. He imagined his ears ringing from the rifle fire, the smell of cordite after each shot. "I don't want to be a soldier."

Tata patted his grandson's thigh. "Don't be silly. You're

only nine. You don't have to be a soldier. Come. Let's make some breakfast."

"I slept in the cave. I need to go back for my machete. Also, Blanca needs some corn." He looked around, and the goat was no longer under the zapote. "Where did she go?"

"I think she went off with the captain. The goat's probably trying to separate the woman from her bootlaces," Tata said. "As for your knife, it'll have to wait. For the moment, they shouldn't know there is a cave."

They went into the cooking shed. To Nicolás the place had a foreignness about it now, as if it belonged to someone else. He could see the whole of the rancho being occupied. His home no longer belonging to him and his grandfather. Tata set about doing what he did each morning: he made a fire, ground coffee beans, and set the beans to brewing in the tin pot. Nicolás went about his own customary duties: he mixed the corn flour with water and made dough. He formed the dough into tortillas and laid them on the hot griddle. They worked in silence, but there was plenty in the air between them. For one, Nicolás rehearsed what he would say when the subject of his coming back to El Retorno arose again. It was only a matter of time. It was Nicolás himself who inadvertently caused the subject to be introduced. "You didn't come home last night, Tata. What happened to you?"

"I was fishing," Tata said. "I ran into them coming back. Or they ran into me, I should say."

"Where was that?"

"Down by the waterfall."

Nicolás knew the spot well. The way the river veered to the left and dropped a bit to form a line of gentle cascades. He often went there and sat upon a particular smooth flat rock and let the water tumble over him. It was like his own private shower. "When they saw you, Tata, what happened?"

"They asked who I was, so I told them. I have nothing to hide." The pot was starting to steam. It let off the appetizing odor of brewing coffee. "Maybe I should've kept my mouth shut."

"Why's that?" Nicolás laid another tortilla on the comal. He flipped the four already browning there.

"Because they said I was just the person they wanted to see. They said that it was to our rancho they were going."

"How did they know about our place?" Nicolás asked again.

"You heard what she said; they have their ways."

The fact was stupefying, but then it was Tata who finally broke the silence. "And you? Why are you here? Where is your mother?"

The truth that Nicolás had dammed up for two days, spilled over the wall of his resolve to keep it hidden. "There was a riot at the cathedral. At the funeral of Monseñor."

"What do you mean a riot?"

"There were bombs and shots and people were running everywhere."

"Where's your mother? What happened to her?"

"We were separated. I tried to run up the steps when she went into the cathedral, but the police wouldn't let me in. I had to run around the side—"

"Wait, wait, wait. Slow down. Tell me slowly what happened."

"Vaya pues." He took a long breath, inhaling the parched corn scent of tortillas roasting on the comal. He remembered everything but would not tell the whole of it. He could not. Why distress Tata now, when, in time, all uncertainties would be made clear again? "We were by Monseñor's casket. Then bombs went off. And gunshots, too. People started running. I was down on the ground. Mamá was lying over me. We were like that for a long time. When the commotion died down, and Mamá crossed into the cathedral, a line of police formed a barricade across the door. They wouldn't let me in. I had to run around the building to find another entrance.

"When I rushed in, half the world was in the cathedral. There were dead people, too. I looked everywhere, but I couldn't find Mamá. She couldn't find me."

"Are you saying you never found her?"

"Yes. But don't worry. She went back to la niña Flor's, but I don't know where that is. That's why I'm here. I came back for the address."

The dog had followed them in, and now a low growl rumbled in its throat. Nicolás turned to see Dolóres and her cohorts stride across the yard. He held on to the ruff of the dog's neck. "Steady, mutt," he said, to keep the animal back.

"Tortillas y café," Dolóres said when she walked in. "The sacred meal of the people."

eleven

About noon, Dolóres's army straggled in: men, women, and three children, the latter belonging to the cook and to the nurse. The people's common item of uniform consisted of their canvas caps. They served as their own pack animals. Upon their backs and heads they balanced tubs and pails and twine-lashed cardboard boxes replete with kitchen provisions: corn flour, lard, powdered milk, beans, rice, sugar, corn, salt, coffee, Maggi brand bouillon cubes, dented pots, long-handled spoons, and kitchen knives. They portaged medical supplies: aspirin, vitamins, antidiarrheal pills and powders, ferrous sulfate, antacids, penicillin, rubbing alcohol, hydrogen peroxide, plastic gloves, bandages, adhesive tape, cotton applicators, sponges, tubing for intravenous procedures, needles, and syringes.

Over the rugged, steep terrain, two men lugged four sacks bulging with coconuts, the water of which provided the sterile fluid for intravenous hydration. Felix, the doctor in charge, toted his own treatment kit in which he carried the instruments that served his field surgery: scissors, clamps, suturing paraphernalia, hemostats, pincers, lancets, and scalpels. Tucked also inside were the precious painkillers and narcotics, the vials of anesthetics. The people carted batteries of several types, a shortwave radio, a two-kilowatt Kohler gasoline generator, a number of five-gallon GI cans filled with gasoline. They carried coils of sisal cording, boxed matches, candles, gunpowder, ammunition, cigarettes, and a battered guitar. Not counting the children, they all shouldered backpacks; the men had machetes as well. Of the group, only ten carried rifles: seven M-16s and three AK-47s, weapons of American and Soviet origin obtained by wresting them from the dead hands of members of the Guardia, or by raiding military depots, or through smuggling them in from Nicaragua. Lidia, an eighteen-year-old guerrillera, put one foot before the other, her belly jutting out in front of her like the bottom of an enormous mixing bowl.

Also carried by them were their wounded. Five of them, transported in the "ambulances of the people." Cocooned in hammocks, they swayed suspended from rigid tree branches spanning the shoulders of the strongest, whose principal aim was to prevent their passengers from caroming into the trees and boulders along the way.

So it was that, without exception, the guerrillas bore the burden of their struggle. They carried also in their hearts the hope that what they did would reward them with a tomorrow far different from the reality they endured today.

Nicolás watched the scenario unfold around him. He sat as unobtrusively as he could under the copinol, his legs drawn up to his chest. To prevent Capitán from attacking, the dog was tethered to the tree trunk. Blanca was another story. The goat roved from group to group, poking her head and nose into what interested her, which proved to be everything.

Nicolás took it all in. He was exhausted from a morning spent hacking down tree branches to be used in new construction. Previous to the task, and on the pretext of having to move his bowels, he stole up the hill behind the rancho and ducked into the cave through the big-stone side and retrieved his machete. It was tucked now between his knees and his chest. He kept an eye on Tata, who went in and out of the rancho following the doctor and Dolóres as they moved things about to suit themselves.

The invasion had arrived only an hour or so before, and already the power plant was up and running. Electric sockets were threaded with 100-watt bulbs, and their cords hung from the room vigas to light the doctor's operating field. The cook—her name was Carmen—had wasted no time. From where Nicolás sat, his back against the tree, he could see, past the shed entrance, the glow of burning coals, the pots of beans and coffee set upon them, the griddle crowded with tortillas. He could hear the cook's hands slapping furiously against each other as she shaped the dough into flat, round cakes. He caught her firm voice as she spoke to her children, two small girls with hair gathered into tails above their ears, their legs and arms streaked with grime. "You both lie down and take a rest," she said to them, motioning with an elbow to a free spot by the wall.

To be sure, no one else was resting. One person worked the radio, trying to tune in the rebel station. A few were setting up a shortwave transmitter, a war-surplus apparatus, banged up and rusty. Others lugged bamboo cane into the yard. They used it to construct lean-tos and frames around which they tightly wove rope to form rudimentary cots. No sooner was one finished than one of the wounded took up the space.

Nicolás's head swam with the sight and sound of so much activity. The urgent commands. The shouts of encouragement. The pounding and hacking and sawing. The bright green smell of newly cut wood. Never had so many occupied this place. He was torn between the novelty of it and who it was that provided it. A small boy wandered up and plunked down beside him, away from Capitán. The boy smelled musky, like the wings of a moth. He had on bright blue shorts and a tan shirt with orange chevrons along the shoulders. He wore a pair of rubber thongs. The boy tucked his legs up to his chest in imitation of Nicolás's stance; he peeked around Nicolás's knees and turned an eye on the dog. "Is he mean?" he asked. "Does he bite?"

Nicolás nodded to both questions, and the boy jerked his head back. Nicolás was sorry he had alarmed him. "His name is Capitán," he said to make it up.

The boy gave a little nod.

"And what's your name?" Nicolás asked.

"Mario."

"How old are you, Mario?"

The boy held up three dirty fingers, then he lowered two and used his index finger to indicate the rancho. "That's my mother in there."

It was the nurse the boy pointed out. She was busy positioning Tata's green table under the harsh light provided by a hanging bulb. She draped the table with a cloth that appeared to have once been a bed sheet. It was imprinted with pink cabbage roses, all of them faded. She hung a plastic bag bulging with amber liquid over the table. The doctor stepped into view. Beyond the door, he had donned a rumpled tunic that long ago had been white. Now he placed a mask around his mouth and nose and tied it behind his head.

The nurse motioned into the yard, and two guerrilleros carried over a hammock enveloping one of the wounded. He appeared to be unconscious. They lifted him to the table.

"They're going to cut him open," Mario said matter-of-factly.

Nicolás saw that it was true. He could see the man's arm stretched out upon the board the nurse had tucked under him. She wore a mask of her own; she bent over his arm. The doctor picked up something shiny and ran the edge of it along the man's belly. Nicolás looked away.

"Which one is your mother?" Mario asked.

"What?"

"Your mother?"

"She's not here," Nicolás said. Two days it had been. What was his mother doing? Did she have her hands full with her charges, the daughters of la niña Flor? A new question came up, and the impact of it startled him. Why hadn't his mother come after him? After all, it wasn't just she who was missing from him. Wasn't he also missing from her? Another thought came, this one more shocking than the first. Roadblocks. Maybe his mother *had* come this way. Maybe it was a roadblock that had prevented their reunion.

"Where is your mother?" Mario asked.

"She's far away."

The man at the radio finally tuned to what he wanted. The rebel radio came on in a loud burst. The reporter was describing Monseñor Romero's funeral. He was telling about the bombs going off, the shots, the stampede. He said that more than 40,000 shoes had been left lying on the plaza. He said that some opportunists had collected them. They had put up stands and were offering the shoes for sale.

Tata came out of the rancho's second room. A stack of

clothing was pressed against his chest. He walked over to Nicolás. "Here are the things from the dresser. They need the dresser for their supplies."

Nicolás wanted to jump up and switch off the radio before Tata could hear the news and start asking more questions.

"Dolóres knows about our cave," Tata said. "Who knows how she found out, but she knows." He handed over the clothing.

Nicolás lowered his legs and laid on them his one extra pair of jeans, two shirts, the T-shirt with the image of the charging bull, the two pairs of socks, and the two undershorts. This was the whole of his wardrobe, scant because in the past year he had shot up like a clump of weeds. His mother had planned to replenish it during his stay in San Salvador.

The radio continued blasting news: "At Monseñor Romero's funeral, thirty-five people died in the plaza. Four hundred and fifty men, women, and children were wounded as well."

"Did you hear that?" Tata said. He went over to the radio and stood next to it as if proximity could improve his understanding of the calamity. Nicolás remained under the tree. There was nothing he could do. The radio man had merely turned a dial and what had come over the airwaves threatened to make real something he was trying hard to deny. Nicolás glanced back to the rancho, to the man on the table. The man's right leg jerked up. To quiet him, the nurse laid a soft hand on his thigh.

• • •

After lunch (bean soup with pitos, rice, tortillas, and coffee), the people allowed themselves some rest. This was usually the time when Tata liked to lay in his hammock and take a snooze, but today he and Tata, and Mario as well, were sitting on the riverbank. Capitán was now accustomed to the newcomers, and he was sprawled out on the sand. It was too early to fish; nevertheless, Tata had brought out his string with a hook on the end. He let the current take it and then he pulled it back, before letting it out again. There were others at the river, too. A guerrillero, the one with the mustache, sat beneath a nearby tree and smoked a cigarette. His rifle was lying across his lap and he seemed lost in reverie. Mario's mother (her name was Rosario and she had two gold front teeth) was knee-deep in the water. She was washing the cabbage-rose table drape, dunking it up and down in the river, then making a loop of it and slapping it hard against a rock.

"You have to go back," Tata said. "I told Dolóres what happened. She also thinks you should go back to your mother."

"Can't we both go, Tata?"

"You know I have to stay."

Nicolás looked out across the river. With the tip of his machete, he made little furrows in the gritty bank.

"You'll leave tomorrow for Tejutla," Tata said. "Dolóres is sending two men with you. They'll see you get on the bus sometime after that."

"Why Tejutla?" He'd never been to Tejutla, but at school he had seen the little red bull's-eye denoting it as a county seat on the teacher's big map.

"There's someone there the men have to visit. Something they have to do." Tata tugged at the line. The hook seemed to have wedged itself among the river rocks.

"Dolóres also says we should stay in the cave tonight."

"You have a cave?" Mario asked.

Nicolás ignored the boy. His head was filled with a coming journey. He recalled the route detailed on the school map. For a short time, they would follow the river, then they would turn south and pass the towns of Cuevitas and San Francisco Morazán. What kind of surprises might these towns provide? "I saved la Virgen from the church," he said, because fear blossomed, and with it the thought of her. "They bombed the church, you know. In El Retorno. I found her statue in the rubble."

"I'm sure she was very grateful," Tata said.

"Yes, she was." Nicolás left it at that. He did not know if Tata would believe the fact that Our Lady had spoken to him. "I put her in the cave. I set her on the ledge by the big stone."

"I want to stay in your cave," Mario said. "I like caves. Bad people can't get you when you're hiding in a cave."

• • •

That night, la Virgen spoke again. The light rays she emitted awakened Nicolás. The niche that held her glowed. He looked around the cave. Tata was wrapped in his hammock, snoring softly. Capitán slumbered under him. Mario lay on a petate, a woven straw mat, next to the big rock. Not one of them awakened. Not one of them heard.

"The lamb, Nicolás," la Virgen said. "Adopt the nature of the lamb and go forward unafraid."

twelve

Gerardo and Elías set out with Nicolás on his journey back to his mother. They left the rancho just before noon so that the men could arrive in Tejutla for a meeting at dusk with a certain Señor Alvarado.

Alvarado worked as an anesthesia technician at the health center there. He had sent word to the rancho that a new shipment of blood had arrived from the capital. Gerardo and Elías were to proceed to Alvarado's house to pick up however many units he had "requisitioned" from the infirmary. At the same time, they were to meet a gringo internationalist, known simply as el Doctor Eddy, who was coming in from Guatemala to volunteer his services. The doctor was traveling under the auspices of the health center. This patronage, arranged by friends of Alvarado, was meant to provide a cover for his bus travels. Once in Tejutla, he would rendezvous with Gerardo and Elías, who would lead him to the rancho. He would stay only long enough to turn a few soldiers into medics. He would give Felix a hand with the wounded.

The three followed the Sumpul, going in an easterly direction, using brush and trees to cover their passing. As usual, Gerardo was dressed in his tattersall shirt and a frayed khaki cap. Elías habitually lifted his own cap and plopped it back on. He followed each off and on with a nervous swipe of two fingers along the fullness of his mustache. The men carried AK-47s and their machetes. Nicolás's knife hung from his waist by a leather thong looped around his wrist. His mother's envelope, with her address printed in her large firm hand, was in his jeans pocket. Stowed in his backpack were the small folding knife, the flashlight, and the lunch Carmen had made for him. Most important, he had packed his mother's shoe and the statue of la Virgen, and the thought of their being with him calmed his anxious heart. Though the Virgin's latest instruction baffled him, he was determined to heed it, so he daydreamed himself as a lamb with Jesús's arm circling his woolly neck.

They stayed well clear of the roads. Gerardo led the way; Elías took up the rear. They zigzagged through the wild terrain, creating a path of their own as the point man hacked at the brush. Nicolás measured his steps to the rhythm of Gerardo's sonorous breathing, to the sound of his machete slashing away at the vegetation. He held up an arm to keep twigs and branches from springing back into his face, while behind him, Elías walked softly. The air was close and hot and opened up the pores, darkening the fabric of their trousers and shirts. Nicolás kept his eye on Gerardo's backpack as if he were following a landmark. He was lulled by the cadence of their steady, sure pace, and in its hypnotic pull he had visions of his mother, of the look on her face when he would stand at her door. He would not stay long with her. This he had decided for himself. Two days in the capital, and then he would return to his grandfather, who needed him to help remind the guerrilleros who it was that owned the rancho.

A stink of putrid flesh wafted up from the river.

"Dead tacuazín," Gerardo said, because opossums were plentiful in the area.

Nicolás cupped a hand over his nose and held his breath.

"I'll take a look," Elías said. Nicolás heard him scrambling down the short incline toward the river on his way to go see.

After a moment, Elías joined them again. "It wasn't that," he said in his own laconic way.

Because warfare placed corpses in unexpected places, neither Nicolás nor Gerardo sought an explanation.

• • •

They paused to gulp down lunch late in the afternoon. Afterward, Gerardo led them to a hamlet on the outskirts of Tejutla. It consisted of one dirt road and seven adobe houses sitting in a row, each leaning into the other as if in commiseration. A meagerness of trees filled the horizon behind the buildings. "Revolution or Death" was scrawled in red paint on an expanse of adobe wall.

"My mother lives in the middle house," Gerardo said, pointing ahead. "She owns the store." While the others peered apprehensively about them, he strode confidently down the road. "Don't worry. It's safe here," he said over his shoulder, and Nicolás understood that Gerardo was addressing his alarm. The look of the place, so quiet and solitary, recalled what he had found at El Retorno—what? a mere three days ago?

Stopping before the opened door of the fourth house, Gerardo called out, "¡Mamá. Mamá!" like a lamb bawling for his mother. At his cries, two dogs came yapping from neighboring houses, and Gerardo kicked out at them to drive them back. Moments later, two women poked their heads past their doorways. When they saw who stood in the street, they called the mutts away but remained at their doors, arms folded over bellies, to see what might transpire.

Calling again as he went, Gerardo entered the house. A clatter arose inside. Nicolás and Elías waited outside, respectful of the exclamations of surprise, of the sobs accentuating the motherly endearments: "Son. My little one. Oh, my little king."

"It's been two years since he's come home," Elías said to Nicolás.

Gerardo appeared at the door and motioned them inside. "Come in! Come in!" his mother, la niña Tencha, urged, standing beside him. She was a tall woman with wizened, dark skin. A white kerchief covered her head and was tied in a long-tailed bow at the nape of her neck. The edge of the cloth stretched across her forehead and was tucked behind her large ears. She wore a green dress sprinkled with tiny flowers. "Don't be shy," she said, inviting them all the way in. She lifted the corner of her apron and wiped her tears.

Her house smelled of rendered lard and candle wax and earth. The dirt floor of its only room was packed down so hard it glistened. A bed frame with coiled springs and no mattress, a chair, and a dresser sat along one wall. The dresser top was crowded with lighted votives and a pedestaled crucifix, with primitive statues and pictures of saints. On the wall above the dresser hung out-of-date calendars with more saintly figures, and several tacked-up family photographs. Looped around all this were chains of paper roses, once pink, it appeared, but now as sooty as the walls.

Across the room sat the woman's enterprise: a glass case so streaked and grimy it was hard to make out the provisions it displayed. Nicolás recognized some items from size and shape alone: Embajadores cigarettes, matchboxes, candles, candies wrapped in waxed paper squares, twists of what might be coffee and sugar and cornmeal. Behind the case, three shelves hung along the wall, each crowded with more provisions. Near the door, on this hot day, a Coca-Cola ice chest hummed industriously. The chest was plugged in at the ceiling fixture, an accomplishment that necessitated three extension cords, these draped loosely along the rafters through bent-over nails. La niña Tencha lifted the lid of the chest and offered them a treat.

When it was his turn, Nicolás plunged his arm into the cold water (it was only that and not ice), swirling it around a bit to cool himself off. Like the others, he captured a bobbing bottle, uncapped it, and gulped down the sweet, fizzy liquid. They stood there awkwardly in the middle of the room with backpacks and machetes and two rifles. Each of them burping softly behind a lifted hand.

Outside, under a wide covered gallery that ran behind all the houses, they sat on chairs facing a clump of powdered trees and a bare hill that, given the odor that wafted from its direction, hid the sight of the latrine. "I was just reviving the fire," la niña Tencha said, pointing to the fire stones overlaid with a clay griddle. "To celebrate your visit, I'm going to fry up a chicken," she announced.

"We can't stay, Mamá," Gerardo said. His cap rested in his lap. His backpack on the ground. His rifle and machete leaned against his thigh. "We're on our way to Tejutla."

"You are not," his mother said. "How long has it been since you've had some fried chicken? That hen's been waiting for my son to come home."

Nicolás could already smell the chicken frying in the pan. He tried to calculate how long it would take to catch it and wring its neck. How long it would take to pluck it and cut it up and fry it.

"It's been quite a while since I've had any chicken," Elías said. "I could go for some chicken."

"You see," Gerardo's mother said. She turned to Nicolás. "Chelito, go fetch that hen. She's out there over the hill somewhere. The big black speckled one, that's the one you want."

Nicolás chased the hen for almost ten minutes. As if knowing her time had come, when Nicolás's shadow fell over her the hen gave a squawk and took off up the hill in a comic swift waddle. Nicolás laughed as she led him straight into a neighbor's back door (perdón, perdón), through the house (not surprisingly, the room looked just like la niña Tencha's), past the front door, and into the street. The scrawny dog that lived there was sprawled under a hammock, and when the hen came flying through, its feathers a puffball of terror, the dog took up the chase, too. Nicolás caught the hen when she put on the brakes and tried to make it around a corner. He picked her up and squeezed her tightly under his arm until he turned her over.

It took la niña Tencha a mere forty minutes to get the chicken into the frying pan. In that time, she scurried around making tortillas, a pot of beans, and coffee. All the while, she kept up a patter. As if they were penitents at mass, Gerardo, Elías, and Nicolás sat in the little chairs lined up in a row and listened to the homily.

"The truth, it's just not the same around here anymore. I don't know what's happening. The whole world's turned upside down. You can't even go to town without fearing for your life. And what good are your children? You have children and you think you're protected. Four men I have. Two girls. You bring them into the world, writhing all the while, and you think they'll grow up to protect you. Especially the men. But that's not the way. Look at your brother Pedro. He ran off into the hills not long after you did. I haven't seen him since. But at least you're sitting here and I can see that you're all right. More than I can say for your brother. Who knows where Pedro is? You remember how it was. He joined the UTC, went to those meetings when I told him not to go. It's a dangerous thing, I told him. But he said, 'Ay, Mamá, you're such a worrier.' As if that would calm my heart. Before long la Guardia came tearing down the door and he ran off into the hills.

"Have you seen him up there? No. Don't answer that. I know how secretive you people are. Truth is, I don't want to know. Better for me if I don't. Your brother Tono, he's another story. He went down to the capital. Went to soldier school. Not too long ago, he came back. Stood there at my door wearing a big grin, a uniform, and boots. 'Son,' I said, 'what has become of you?' And he said, 'I'm a soldier, Mamá.' I had to turn my head so he wouldn't see me cry. Ay, we're a family divided, that's what we are. You and Pedro. Tono and Juan. You knew about Juan, right? Maybe you didn't. You've been away so long. Juan took one look at Tono's uniform, one look at those sturdy boots, and it was little feet, watch me now. He went off to the capital. Got boots of his own. A uniform and rifle, too. But that one's not come strutting back. That one's stayed away. Every now and then, one of the neighbors says, 'Saw your boy Juan. He looks mighty fine in his uniform.' It gives a mother pause. To have four boys and all of them soldiers of some kind. What kind of thing is that? Ay, Dios Santo.

"You heard about Nadia? My precious little girl. Five

months along and sticking out to here. The security forces, they ambushed her. Up the road somewhere. Neighbor came running. 'Nadia's up there,' the neighbor said. And you could tell by the way he put it, you could tell by the way he couldn't lift his eyes, that the news would be bad. Truth is, they ripped her open. Sons of bitches, they just ripped her apart. Wasn't enough to kill her like she was some kind of pig. No. They had to rip her open and pull the baby out. Left it lying in the road. A little bundle of blood. He was a boy. I saw this for myself. His little peepee, it was as big as this. Oh, well. It's probably for the best. Another boy brought into the world. ¿Pa'que? What for? For joining the army? For joining the people in the hills? Ay, Virgen Santa.

"All I have now is Margarita. She works in Tejutla. Comes to see me every few weeks. I have you, of course, but you I haven't seen for two years. So all I really have is my Margarita. Do you realize your sister's sixteen? A señorita now. So pretty. Ay, but what good is pretty? What does it get you but a baby in the belly? A bloody dead baby tossed into the road."

thirteen

They could see Señor Alvarado's house from the trees. The front wall was painted a shy shade of lilac, which is how they recognized it. La casa lila was how it had been described. Gerardo and Elías and Nicolás eased out, stealthy as pumas, from under a stand of olive trees, where they had been waiting for darkness. To lower their profile, the men tucked the butts of their rifles under their armpits and clasped the barrels to their sides. The temperature had fallen in concert with the shade of night, but still it was hot. The street lamp on the corner threw a coin of light onto the middle of the street. Through opened windows and over patio walls wafted the odor of peppers, onions, and tomatoes, of meat smoking over coals. Somewhere near, a radio played a ballad: "Oh, my love, try not to love me so much."

At Alvarado's door, Gerardo glanced up and down the street. He lifted the iron knocker and gave a soft *raprap*. The door swiftly opened, as if the person who opened it, a stocky, middle-aged man with no hair atop his head but with eyebrows like two woolly worms, had been waiting there all day. They exchanged words that Nicolás could not catch but that gained them admission.

They crossed a short concrete patio and passed through a second door and into the house itself. The light of two lamps illuminated a combined dining and living room. Alvarado led them to a table. Gerardo and Elías dropped their backpacks, propped up their rifles and machetes, and pulled up chairs. With a long sigh, Elías lit a cigarette. A bowl piled with bright pebble-skinned fruit occupied the center of the table. Nicolás thought they looked like tangerines, but he had never had the luck to taste one. Though there were four chairs, he allowed the adults their positions at the table. He set his own things down and took a chair away from the others, next to a refrigerator that was backed against the wall. El señor Alvarado asked if they were thirsty. Before anyone could respond, he opened up the refrigerator and fished around in the door shelves and brought out a pair of Pilsners and a Coca-Cola. Nicolás felt the rush of cool air as the refrigerator stood open. He noted that the inside shelves were stacked with vials and bottles. Rusty-looking fluid filled a large number of plastic bags.

"Who's the kid?" Alvarado asked, handing Nicolás the Coca-Cola but putting the question to the men.

"He's from up in the hills. We're going to put him on the bus." Gerardo took a long drink of beer and his Adam's apple bobbed up and down.

"Where's he going?"

"San Salvador."

"Not tonight he isn't," Alvarado said. "The bridge at the dam was blown up."

"When was that?" Elías asked, cigarette smoke curling from his nostrils.

"This morning. Now there are roadblocks at Las Cañas. There's some even over in Chalatenango." Alvarado set his bottle down with a dull thud on the table. "Who knows how long it'll be before they let the buses through."

At the news, Nicolás felt the blood drain away from his head. His thirst disappeared, and he set his bottle down with a thunk on the floor beside him.

Gerardo said, "What about el gringo? El Doctor Eddy?"

"He's coming in from Honduras," Alvarado said. "The bus from La Palma should be all right. It should arrive within the hour. But I tell you what, the gringo won't be getting here a moment too soon."

"What am I going to do?" Nicolás said, surprising himself that he had actually voiced the very thing that troubled him.

"Looks like you're not going anywhere for now," Gerardo said.

"But my mother . . ." Nicolás could feel his bottom lip start to quiver. In an effort to control himself, he let it go at that.

"What's wrong with your mother?" Alvarado asked, addressing Nicolás for the first time.

"Mí mamá . . ." It was useless. He could not go on. Tears welled up, and he lowered his chin onto his chest.

"His mother was in that mess at Monseñor's funeral," Gerardo explained. "The kid was, too. They were separated and he couldn't find her, so he went home to his grandfather. That's where our people are, at the grandfather's rancho. Now the kid's trying to go back to the capital and find his mother."

Nicolás heard Gerardo's explanation. Would what happened at the cathedral ever make any sense?

"Come here," Alvarado said.

Nicolás lifted his head to make sure it was him that the man addressed. "Me?" he asked.

"Yes, you. Come over here." Alvarado pulled the last chair away from the table. "Sit here." He had sausagelike fingers. He tapped the chair seat with one of them.

Nicolás did as he was told.

"Where does your mother live?"

Nicolás pulled out the envelope his mother had addressed with a thick-leaded pencil. The envelope was damp and wrinkled from being inside his pocket. He laid it on the table, smoothed it out with his hand. "This is where she works."

Alvarado studied the envelope. "What does she do, your mother?"

"She's a nursemaid. At la niña Flor's."

"I see." Alvarado furrowed his brow and the woolly worms of his eyebrows inched closer together.

Nicolás risked interrupting Alvarado's train of thought. "I want to get on the bus and go to la niña Flor's. I want to see my mother. That way she'll know that I'm safe."

"I'm sure your mother's worried about you," Alvarado said.

Nicolás nodded. "She's worried."

"Well, why don't you write her a letter and tell her that you're fine."

"A letter?"

"Yes, you have an envelope there, and it's ready to be posted. All you need is a sheet of paper, a pencil, and you can write her a note."

"Write her a note?" What a splendid idea. This was something that had never crossed his mind.

Alvarado scraped back his chair. He crossed the room and went to a small desk. He slid out a drawer and pawed through it. He came back to the table with what was needed. "Here," he said, laying pencil and paper down. "You write to your mother."

Nicolás sat up straight. It was as if he were back in school, and la señora Menjivar (may she rest in peace) was handing out an assignment. He ran his palm down the side of his jeans to dry the moistness. He bunched his fingers around the pencil and set the point upon the paper. He felt the tip of his tongue slipping past his lips, an indication that he was ready. He wrote "Dear Mamá" in block letters slanting downward, something he could not control. He continued precisely in the way that he'd been taught. The words formed themselves in his mind as he remembered them: "I hope that when this reaches you, it finds you well." The going was slow. There were words he could not spell, so he rolled the sounds of them around in his head and relayed them to his fingers as best he could. He told his mother he was well. That he had taken the bus back to el rancho. That Tata was well. Capitán, too. He told her that he would see her soon. "Ya te bua' ver," was the way he wrote that. He did not write about the roadblocks. He did not write about Gerardo and Elías and Dolóres, nor about the swarm of people gathered at the rancho. He ended the letter with. "Don't be afraid. From your son Nicolás." Satisfied, he lifted his head, passed his hand over the paper as if with a palm he could make it all more clear.

"Finished?" Alvarado asked, glancing over.

"Ah," Nicolás said, because he remembered one last thing. He bent his head over the paper again and added, "La birgen mesta cuidando. Our Lady is taking care of me."

"There," he said to Alvarado. "Finished."

Alvarado turned his thick wrist over and looked at his watch. "The bus from La Palma should be getting in any minute. I'm walking down to the terminal to meet the gringo." He rose from his seat. "You boys pack up that blood. Pack up all the supplies I've stored in the refrigerator." He motioned through the windows. "There are Styrofoam boxes out in the patio. String too. There's ice in the freezer to keep the blood cool. When I get back with the gringo, you must leave at once."

Gerardo and Elías stood, and Nicolás did as well. He stuffed the letter into the envelope. Licked the envelope closed. Held it in his hand.

"Chele, want a tangerine?" Alvarado asked.

Nicolás shrugged.

"Get yourself one."

Nicolás reached for the one at the top of the pile, for he was not bold enough to dig through them looking for the best one. To free his hands, he tucked his mother's letter under his arm. He slipped the skin off the fruit, amazed at how easily it fell away. He used a finger to break the fruit apart, and it fell open like a little orange cup, giving off a sharp fresh essence all its own. He ate it all in three bites. It was very sweet. A dribble of juice ran down his chin, and it suddenly shamed him that they could see his hungry eagerness. He lifted his shoulder and wiped his mouth against his shirt.

"Take another one," Alvarado said, "there's plenty." Then he turned to the men. "The kid's going with me. On the way to the bus, we'll pass the post office. I'm going to show him where I'll mail his letter in the morning."

Years later, Nicolás would remember that night. Almost

every detail of it. Leaving the house and the surprising look
of an undisturbed street. The added miracle of the little pharmacy on the corner. FARMÁCIA EL BUEN PASTOR, the sign
read. It featured a drawing of Jesús holding a crook-end
staff, a herd of black-faced lambs swarming around him.
And Nicolás would remember the velvet air pressing down
on his bare arms. The steady sure steps sounding at his side.
In one hand, the feel of his mother's letter, a form of assur-
ance restored. In the other hand, like an undeserved reward,
a second tangerine. Throughout his life, it was unsolicited
kindness that the scent of tangerines recalled.

fourteen

Because his mother was Mexican, el Doctor Eddy was only half a gringo. He spoke adequate Spanish, which was a good thing, because when Gerardo said, "Vámos ir a la casa de mí Mamá," and, once they were on the way, "En el camino, no hay que hablar," the doctor understood that they were going to Gerardo's mother's house and that on the trip they were not to say a word. Eddy was a large, muscular man with freckled skin and a head of thick blond hair. Hair sprouted from the V of his shirt collar; it matted his arms. He was a jovial sort, Nicolás could tell. When he got off the bus, carrying the stuffed backpack and the black leather bag, he shook hands with Alvarado and then with Nicolás, an amazing thing for an adult.

Near midnight they reached la niña Tencha's, and this second arrival surprised and pleased the old woman as much as their earlier visit had. They set the Styrofoam coolers (there were four of them) on the floor and el Doctor Eddy took la niña Tencha's hand, thanking her for her shelter and hospitality, and she widened her eyes at the fact that it was Spanish that came from the big chele's mouth. Gerardo explained to his mother that they would remain overnight. That, for safety's sake, they would not leave until dusk the following day. He also explained that the coolers they had carried from Tejutla were filled with medications and that these must be kept cool, and so the Coca-Cola chest was emptied and units of blood and vials of muscle relaxant and anesthesia took the place of bobbing bottles.

The men arranged themselves on the dirt floor of the gallery, allowing the old woman her privacy inside. Nicolás curled himself around his backpack. He held the statue of la Virgen tucked within. His arms ached from steadying the box he had carried on his head for over an hour. He tried not to think of the trip back to the rancho, of the hours it would take to struggle up and down the hills before they reached home. Instead, he imagined his letter wending its way from the post office all the way to la niña Flor's door. He fell asleep attempting to puzzle out the unfathomable journey the envelope would take before it appeared in his mother's hand.

The odor of brewing coffee awakened them all. La niña Tencha was bustling about her cooking spot, readying their breakfast. As was her bent, she prattled as she worked.

She said, "During hard times, you have to take advantage. After I woke up, before I started the fire, I went down the street. I told the neighbors we have a doctor in our midst, a real miracle from la Virgen Santa and from God. I hope you don't mind, Dr. Eddy, but soon the people will be lining up out here in back. In peaceful times there's the health center in Tejutla we can visit, but these days it's not prudent to be out on the open road. Too many sought relief there for a throbbing head or an aching belly only to lose their life in an ambush along the way. I told the neighbors to respect your time and not to overwhelm you with complaints, and God knows we have complaints. But you look like you can stand up to the barrage. I can see you are a good man, a young doctor, but a good one, and we are thankful for that. Like I said, during hard times like these, you have to take advantage."

True to her word, the people arrived soon enough. For such a small hamlet, lacking even a name, it contained a surprising number of women, old men, and children. El Doctor Eddy sat on a wide bench someone had dragged out under the gallery, his black bag open and handy beside him. He enlisted Nicolás as his helper, though the only help he could give was to keep the people in line, the dogs shooed, and children distracted during their examinations. The most common complaints were stomach and chest ailments. There were also headaches and earaches.

"My stomach hurts," a young woman said when she stepped up to take her turn. She appeared to be six or seven months pregnant. She cupped her hands over her belly as she explained to the doctor how much it ached.

"Have you been bleeding?" the doctor asked.

"No," she said, jerking her neck back as if the question were absurd.

"From below. Have you been bleeding from below?"

She reddened at the question. "No," she said.

"What have you been eating?"

The woman grew pensive. "Nothing," she said at length. "Just my tortillas and my beans. My coffee. That and green mangoes."

"Green mangoes?"

The woman's eyes brightened. "I love green mangoes. I eat them with salt."

El Doctor Eddy dug around in his bag and extracted a large plastic bottle of Tums. He shook six dusty-colored tablets out onto his palm and handed them over to the woman. "Take two right now. Then if your stomach still hurts, take another one in four hours."

"Which color?"

"Take the pink ones first. Then the yellow ones. Then the green. Chew them up good."

The woman beamed. She popped the pink tablets into her mouth. Pocketed the rest. "Gracias, Doctor," she said, turning shy again.

An old man with a festering sore on his ankle was next in line. Even before he lifted the edge of his trouser leg, you could smell his affliction. Eddy asked Nicolás to boil up some water. When it was ready, the doctor used gauze squares to clean out the sore. He worked quickly and efficiently, the sun falling on his arms and turning the hair on them gold. The old man had propped his leg on the bench, and he stood ramrod, his mouth twisted in stoic forbearance. Nicolás did not draw away from the angry-looking flesh and the white little worms that wiggled in it. He watched carefully as the doctor tweezed the worms out with a pincer and then covered the sore with a dark pungent ointment. Watched as he wrapped the ankle with a clean new bandage.

"You need to keep this leg dry," Eddy said to the old man. "Let the sore dry up."

The man gave a little laugh that was more like a grunt. "I fish for a living," he said.

"Do you fish in the river?" Eddy asked.

The old man rolled his eyes. "Where else?"

"Well, fish like a crane," Eddy said. "Keep this leg folded up."

"What's wrong with the river?" Nicolás asked.

"River water's dirty. It'll keep the sore infected." Eddy shook a few aspirins into the man's palm. "These are for when the thing pains you."

"Nothing pains me," the old man said. He thanked the doctor and went off. He was only steps away when a woman down the line spilled out her complaints to him. He listened and handed her his aspirins.

"My baby's burning up with fever," the next woman said. She held a fitful baby with a nose running green snot and with glassy-looking eyes.

Dr. Eddy placed a hand on the baby's forehead. "I don't even need my thermometer."

"I bet her temperature is forty centigrade. Maybe forty-one," the woman said.

El Doctor Eddy nodded.

Nicolás thought the baby was going to die. A temperature that reached over forty was a very dire thing. La niña Ursula's baby had died. He was a boy two months old. "He had a forty-one temperature," Ursula said when she told Nicolás about it. Now Nicolás stood near a mother with desperation in her eyes. She held her baby and the doctor attempted to have the child take sips of sugar water in which he'd mashed up half an aspirin. Every time he brought the cup near the baby's mouth, the baby moved its head away. "If only we had something she could suck," Eddy said.

Nicolás thought of the tangerine that was in his backpack. He was saving it for a treat. He brought it out and peeled it and pulled off one little section and made a small rip in the end of it. "Here," he said, and placed the fruit between the baby's lips. It took only a moment for the baby to take to the fruit. Between sucks, the mother got her daughter to drink the water. When the cup was empty, and it was time for an injection, Nicolás held the baby while the mother turned away as Eddy swabbed a spot on the baby's brown buttock. When the needle struck, the baby turned her face to Nicolás and let out a snotty yell. When the worst was over, the mother took her baby back and clasped her to her bosom. "Ya ya ya," she said, bouncing up and down on her heels to comfort her.

Nicolás wiped his face down the length of his arm. He handed the mother the rest of the tangerine.

"You're a good helper," el Doctor Eddy said. "If you want, when we get to the rancho, I'll teach you a few things."

Nicolás shrugged, trying hard to conceal his delight.

fifteen

Nicolás was hauling water up the hill when the fever finally stopped him. In the three days he had been home, his arms and legs felt achy, but this he attributed to the toil of toting a heavy box of medications uphill all the way from Tejutla. Now he thought his head would explode. He set the bucket down, steadying it with a leg, but water still slopped over the edge. Little Mario, the nurse's son, stared up at him. "What's wrong with you?" the boy asked. He pointed to the sweat pouring down Nicolás's face. Nicolás wiped his brow. It was as if a spigot had opened up along his forehead and over his upper lip. From one moment to the next, profound exhaustion had overtaken him. "It's hot," he said, but he feared it was more than that.

He plodded up to the rancho, Mario trailing behind. Nicolás carried the bucket into the cooking shed, where Carmen was making lunch. She stopped stirring the beans in the pot. "What's wrong with you?"

Virgen Santa, did it show? "My head hurts."

"You've been out in the sun too long. Look at you. You look flushed. Go sit under the trees. It's cooler there. The

89

soup will be ready soon, and I'll bring you some." She let the spoon rest against the rim of the bean pot and grabbed Mario's hand. "And you, you give the boy some peace. Go sit in the corner with the girls for a while." The cook's oldest daughter was entertaining her little sister with the dried husk of a cicada she had pulled off a tree. She was using one of the kitchen knives to slice up the husk and see what was inside. Mario hunched down beside the girls. "Give me that," he said, and snatched the knife away.

Nicolás went outside. Maybe that's all it was, too much sun. Tata had sent him out to the little field to gather fodder for the goat. Nicolás and Mario had made four trips. Then there was the water to haul up and down the path under the strong sun. But why did all his bones feel as if they were broken? He plunked down under the copinol, his favorite place because it offered the best view of things. He leaned his throbbing head against the tree trunk and tried to distract himself.

He could no longer see directly into the rooms of the rancho where the doctors performed surgery and where the newly operated-upon regained consciousness. During his absence, the people had built an overhung gallery along the side of the hut. The rope cots they had constructed when they first arrived were placed there, all of them occupied by the wounded. Chema, the man whom Felix had opened up days ago, was lying there. His stomach incision was not healing properly. It oozed pus and was malodorous, and flies swarmed over it. Most of the time, Chema lay in a stupor and moaned. Now that new supplies had arrived, the IV hanging from an overhead viga was filled with glucose and not with coconut water as it had been before. On another bed, beside him, Samuel lay stoically with a leg blown apart by shrapnel. In an effort to save the leg, Dr. Eddy and Felix had spent two hours picking bomb fragments from the wound and reconstructing what was left of Samuel's femur; luckily for him there were fresh anesthetics and antibiotics. While he recovered, he was a placid man. Dr. Eddy, with Nicolás's help, had rigged up a narrow wooden ramp to keep his leg elevated. The doctor had strung up a rope past a viga and tied a rock around the end, a makeshift counterweight to keep the bone aligned. Samuel never complained about the tugging pressure. Periodically, he reached a hand across the short distance between him and Chema's bed to keep flies from settling on his partner's wound.

Outside the house, under the trees and beneath the newly built lean-tos, the daily business of revolution continued. One man attended to the static-sputtering radio; another tweaked the dial of a portable, searching the popular radio for the latest news; a circled group of soldiers listened attentively to Dolóres discuss tactics for their next attack; Lidia, oblivious to her bulging belly, called out the letters of the alphabet as she taught some of them to read.

Under one of the lean-tos, Tata bent over a rough-hewn table making firebombs. In addition to fishing for the group's meals, his other assignment was bomb construction. Elías had taught him. First, Tata scraped off the phosphorus heads of matches and ground them up into a powder. Then he heaped a pinch or two of powder upon a square of aluminum foil. He closed the foil tightly. Pressed the packet against the base of an ordinary candle, trimmed to a calculated length to act as a timing device. Lastly, he jammed the candle into the neck of a bottle containing gasoline. When the bomb was used, a guerrillero settled on a target and set the candle down. Lastly, he touched a match to the wick and walked away. A short time later—*kabum!*—a conflagration.

Carmen came out of the cooking shed. She was a chunky

woman, with strong knotty legs that ended in a pair of turquoise flip-flops that slapped smartly against the ground as
she walked. In one hand, she carried a bowl of soup. With
the other she hiked up the strap that had fallen over her
meaty shoulder. "Here, drink this," she said to Nicolás.
"Fish soup made with your grandfather's catch."

Nicolás muttered a thank-you, and accepted the soup.
He took a few sips, letting its steam wash over his face. He
inhaled its fragrance but felt his stomach turn at the smell
of it. He forced half the soup down but put the bowl aside
when his face erupted in a new wave of perspiration. He
struggled to his feet and staggered up the back hill, seeking
the shortest route to the cave. He passed the lean-to where
Felix and Eddy and Rosario, the nurse with the two gold
teeth, were holding a workshop for five guerrilleros who
would serve as medics. Over Tata's protests that he practice
his letters and numbers, it was with the doctors that Nicolás
preferred to be. But not today. Today he needed his hammock. He needed his Virgencita, nestled in her niche, to
watch over him.

• • •

In the cave, he collapsed into the hammock, his body both
feverish and chilled. Comforted by the scent of loam and by
the gentle light, his mind wandered to pleasant thoughts. He
found himself with his mother again. They were on their way
to Arcatao, as they had been a year before when Monseñor
Romero had visited the town. He had come to celebrate mass
and to speak to the people, to give them courage and to
rekindle their hopes for justice. Nicolás's mother, being a
Romero devotee, had fetched Nicolás for the occasion. Basilio Fermín, a man who was almost as old as Tata and who
was la niña Flor's chauffeur, arrived with Lety that day.

Now Nicolás relived the time: the three of them joining the band of faithful along the open trail. Their camaraderie. Their joyful expectation. The popular song they sang as they ambled along: "And if they want my blood, I'll give them my blood. I'll gladly give it for the exploited people of my country."

Cocooned in the hammock, Nicolás pictured once more his mother's sweet face. She was rapt as they stood before the little church listening to Monseñor tell the crowd he had been detained. "Look, on the way here, I was threatened, but it was only a test." He went on to beseech them, "Let this fact not dismay you, but may it give you strength. Press forward in your struggle."

During mass, Monseñor's imploration had been underscored by the angelic voice of a woman intoning the "Ave María"; it was as if Our Lady herself had called out to them.

On the trip home, the people spent the night along the banks of the Sumpul. In his hammock, dreaming with fever, Nicolás glimpsed their bright fires again. He caught the fragrance of coffee and corn. He recalled the people's stories. Their newfound hope. He watched Basilio Fermín prop himself against a tree. Watched him carve a wooden animal from a small block of wood.

And he heard his mother say, "Look, it's a lamb."

"The lamb is the symbol of the lost," Basilio Fermín added.

Nicolás asked, "Who is lost?"

"We are all lost," Mamá responded.

In the cave, Nicolás forced his eyes open. Someone was shaking the hammock. He lifted his head and saw that it was Mario.

"What's wrong with you?" the boy said. "I looked all over and you were gone."

"I don't feel good." Nicolás's head fell back against the hammock strings. The movement was utterly exhausting.

"I'm getting my mother," Mario said.

Nicolás was too tired to argue.

Rosario shook Nicolás awake again; this time he couldn't lift his head.

She laid a hand on his brow. "My God, you're burning up. I'm getting Dr. Eddy."

Nicolás was too achy to argue.

Minutes later, the cave filled with people: Rosario and Mario again. Tata and Capitán and Eddy. Tata laid his big hand, smelling of unstruck match heads, upon Nicolás's forehead. "He's burning up," he said.

Eddy said, "Give me a little room." And then, "I tell you what. Why don't you all step outside. When I'm finished looking him over, you can come back inside." He then knelt beside the hammock. "How do you feel?"

"It hurts."

"What hurts?"

"My head. All my bones. My bones feel like they're broken."

"Here, let me take your temperature. Open your mouth."

The stiff rod slid between his lips; his teeth clamped down on glass.

"Don't bite on it. Just let it rest against your tongue. There. That's good."

The gringo waited, kneeling, then extracted the glass rod. "Mmm," Eddy said.

"What?"

"You have quite a fever. It's one hundred and three. But that's in Fahrenheit." The gringo stood and turned toward the tunnel. "I'll be right back. You're very dehydrated. We need to start you on some fluids."

Nicolás closed his eyes. In his ears echoed the shuffling sounds Eddy made as he proceeded, hunched over, down the tunnel. Nicolás laid both hands against his cheeks. It was true; he was burning up. His hands were as hot as his face. One hundred and three of temperature, when forty-one was enough to strike a person dead. Though it took a great effort, he lifted his head and looked toward la Virgen. Her blue gown, her chipped little crown, her one intact arm, mixed together and flowed before him like a mirage. "If you're ready to take me," he whispered in her direction, "I suppose I'm ready to go."

· · ·

Dying took time. Dying caused your head to swirl with the hum of the insects and with images that made you dizzy: your mother being dragged between two men with green crosses stamped upon their helmets, your mother lifting a bare foot to stop them, her standing and rearranging herself as if she had been on an amusement park ride. Your mother's wide grin. Her running to embrace you. "I bet you thought that I was dead!" your mother exclaiming.

Dying was being trapped inside a tunnel like the one leading down to the river, but this one with no entrance and no exit. This tunnel was hot and there was no air and the walls of it shrank around you as you rushed back and forth trying to escape.

Dying was the wail of la Ziguanaba calling out to you even though it was the middle of the day. La Ziguanaba on the riverbank, warming herself in the sun. La Ziguanaba reaching into the tunnel to pluck you out with pointy red fingers.

But dying brought also Our Lady's voice of reason. "I am with you, Nicolás. See the light my hands extend. Be calmed by the light. You are protected by my light."

Nicolás moaned, "Yes, I see it," though he had no strength to lift his eyes toward the niche.

"There, there, my son," someone said, and it was Tata's voice.

"Tata. Where are you?" When he was trapped in the suffocating tunnel, he had heard Tata calling. Over and over, as if Nicolás were his little lost lamb.

"I'm here beside you. Capitán's here, too. Feel him under you?"

"Umm," Nicolás uttered, though all he could feel were his own shattering bones.

"The doctor put a needle in your arm and there's medicine in a bag going into you. Keep your arm straight, son. Don't move your arm."

"Umm."

Time was a long river, and he floated on its surface, drifting down the middle, keeping away from the banks where death and danger lurked. From time to time a damp rag was pressed against his forehead. From time to time Tata's broad hand cupped his neck and lifted his head toward the rim of a glass. "Here," he said, "you need to drink lots of water."

Four days later, when Eddy took his temperature and it had dropped to ninety-eight, Nicolás was pronounced well. He hobbled from the cave, stepping out into a sun so bright it hurt his eyes. He came down the hill, leaning stiffly against Tata. Fifty-seven numbers above the dreaded forty-one and he was still among the living. It was Our Lady who had carried out the miracle. She who would keep him well until the number was right.

sixteen

The wooden lamb, and a lion, too, both of which Basilio Fermín had carved, Nicolás placed in the niche next to Our Lady's statue after he was well. Until he was sick and the feverish dreams had come, he had forgotten these little gifts. Forgotten Basilio Fermín himself, his dark face, long and drawn down as a hound's.

Nicolás told Tata he had sent a letter to his mother; he said that el señor Alvarado had delivered it to the post office in Tejutla. Nicolás quoted what he had written by heart. He said to Tata, "Maybe after Mamá receives the letter, after the bridge at the dam is repaired and it's safer to travel, maybe then Basilio Fermín will bring her back. Like when they came and we went to Arcatao to see Monseñor."

"May God will it," Tata replied, storm clouds in his eyes.

Tonight, he and Tata were hanging slack in their hammocks. Beneath them, Mario slept on the straw mat by the big stone at the cave entrance. It had been a taxing day. Samuel's leg had taken a bad turn. He had spiked a fever and become delirious, no longer capable of keeping the flies

from settling on Chema, who lay a bed away. That job had
passed to Nicolás. For hours he had fanned a cardboard
square back and forth across Chema's bandaged wound.
Chema was conscious now, but despondent. He stared past
his feet to a point across the yard where the rebel radio
crackled out news and information. From his vantage point,
Nicolás kept an eye on Samuel—and on Felix, who, from
time to time, bent over Samuel to take his temperature. The
doctor had to place the glass rod under Samuel's armpit, for
fear, he said, that if he slipped it into his mouth, Samuel
would snap it in two. Each time Felix read the thermometer,
Nicolás asked the same question, "How high is it?"

"Thirty-eight centigrade," Felix would say, or "Thirty-
nine," or "Thirty-nine and a half."

The rising numbers alarmed Nicolás and heightened his
anxiety. Periodically, he laid a quick palm against his cheek,
feeling for heat. After a time, he said to Felix, "Do you think
you can take my temperature?" It had been five days since
he had been ill. Surely his own numbers had diminished
by now.

"Why would you want that?" Felix said.

Nicolás shrugged. How could he share the baffling com-
plexity of his emotions? He had been so close to death, and
la Virgen Milagrosa had reached out with her light to save
him. He believed this with all his strength. Still, he could not
help but want more proof. Something reassuringly tangible,
like his own body temperature all the way down to normal.

Across from Chema's bed, Samuel whined, "Mámi,
where are you? Don't leave me, Mámi."

"Poor guy. Calling for his mother." Felix shook his
head. "If his temperature goes much higher, we'll have to
amputate."

"So," Nicolás said, "do you think you can take it?"

"It won't be easy. Amputations can be gruesome things."

"No," Nicolás said. "Take my temperature."

"Oh, for God's sakes! Come here." Felix swabbed the rod with alcohol and laid it atop Nicolás's tongue. Nicolás closed his lips carefully around it. He kept very still. He silently prayed, Santa María, Madre de Dios.

"There," Felix said, taking a look after what seemed an eternity. "Thirty-seven centigrade. You are a normal kid."

The tightened muscles in Nicolás's legs relaxed with his relief. "I knew that," he had replied.

Thinking about it, he smiled to himself in the darkness of the cave. He closed his eyes, waiting for sleep. Tomorrow, very early, he would be leading Elías and Gerardo to El Retorno. Samuel needed his leg amputated after all, but nowhere in the camp was there a saw with which to do it. There were machetes, of course, plenty of them, and they would do the job if no saw could be had. But it was a saw el Doctor Eddy preferred. A saw is more precise, he explained. A saw can be controlled. To amputate with a machete, you'd have to give a good whack. A machete whistling down toward Samuel's thigh was a terrible thing to contemplate, so Nicolás had told Dolóres about the saw that customarily hung from a peg on the wall of Ursula's gallery. "She uses it to cut up the wood for the ovens. She doesn't like using a machete. She says a saw is easier."

"Well, then, that does it," Dolóres had said. "You're the one to fetch it."

Nicolás pictured himself in El Retorno again. Had some of the people come back to town? La niña Ursula to her tortilla-making place? Doña Paulina to her store? And what of Emilio Sánchez? If relatives came looking for him, and they happened upon the bombed-out shell of his place, how would they know to find him at the church? The question caused Nicolás to recognize he had a similar problem. If Tata and he were separated, as they had been that first day when Nicolás arrived from San Salvador, how would they ever find each other? "Tata. Tata, wake up."

"What's wrong?" Tata grumbled.

"If something happened to us, Tata, if we were separated, how would we find each other? I'm scared, Tata, I think . . ."

"Wait, wait, wait," Tata said. "My God, I was sound asleep."

Patiently as he could, Nicolás let a moment pass, then he said, "Are you awake now, Tata?"

"I'm awake. What's the matter?"

Nicolás slowly explained: "If something happened and we were separated, where would I find you, Tata? Where would you find me?"

"That's a very good question," Tata said at length.

"Then let's agree on a place."

They discussed the possibilities: the cave itself, the bend downriver where the waterfall was, where Tata caught fish. The refugee camp, way past that spot and across into Honduras. In the end, they decided on El Retorno. If ever they were separated, they each would try to make his way back to the town and to the church.

"The bombs destroyed half of it," Nicolás said, "but the niche where la Virgen was, that wall still stands." He hesitated, but only for a moment, before adding, "La Virgen said she would protect me. She told me not to be afraid."

"Well, there you have it," Tata replied, "Our Lady doesn't lie. If the need arises, we'll meet at her wall." Tata cleared his throat a few times, as if settling himself back down again. "So, go to sleep, Nico. Quiet now."

"Okay," Nicolás said, relieved that his first mention of la Virgen speaking had not prompted Tata's disbelief.

• • •

There was no saw at Ursula's. The place on the gallery wall where it usually hung was bare. The house itself had been stripped of its possessions. Ransacked, as the little store had been, and the pharmacy as well. Both doors blown open. The interiors in shambles: shelving down, glass display cases shattered. Both places robbed of everything worth taking.

When they arrived at Ursula's, Nicolás inspected the front room (the corn dough in the tubs was as hard as stone). Through the back door he crossed the patio to Ursula's one-room house. It stood soundless and vacant, just as it had been two weeks ago, when he had first come through it. But now there was chaos, the same as what he had seen up and down the street, and it all spoke of evil. Exactly who had come to take what little there was to take?

Nicolás returned to the street where Elías and Gerardo stood under the eave of a building, keeping watch, out of the sun. Nicolás explained the problem.

"Who else would have a saw?" Gerardo asked. Just yesterday he had changed out of his tattersall shirt. Today, he sported one of shiny brown polyester. He had rolled the sleeves up, two folds past the elbows.

"We have to find one and get out of here," Elías said. "We don't have to guess who was here before us." He lifted his cap and quickly set it back on his head again.

Nicolás tried thinking past the comment. He tried to see past the image of pillaging soldiers or marauding Guardia.

"Emilio Sánchez had a saw. But then, his place was burned out in the bombing."

"Saws don't burn," Gerardo said, and the three of them trotted over to what remained of Emilio's shop. While his companions poked hastily through the rubble with the tips of their boots, Nicolás went on up the street to see if Emilio himself might be at the church. Nicolás stood at the bottom of the hill looking up to the building, still surprised to see its state of ruin. The rents in the earth caused by the bombing had softened somehow, but the huge conacaste that was split down the trunk looked sadder now. The leaves on the branches resting against the altar had curled tightly into brown cylinders.

"Emilio!" Nicolás called, hesitant to go nearer. "Are you there?"

When no answer came, Nicolás looked down the hill at his drab little town. The evil that lurked there in its lifeless streets made tears well up, so he lifted his machete and whacked at the dull, stiff grass rising past his boot tops. From below, the *brrrtt!* of an automatic came, and then more rifle fire. Nicolás flattened himself on the ground. He was out in the open. An easy target. The schoolroom was on the corner. He jumped up and ran toward it, knife in hand. He rushed inside, almost stumbling over its broken tables and chairs. He backed against the wall, using it as a shield, and edged toward a window in the direction the shots seemed to be coming from. He crouched under the sill, listening to the barrage of rifle fire beyond it. When the gunfire stopped, Nicolás caught the sound of his heart thumping in his ears. After a moment, he stood, lifting his eyes past the windowsill.

Elías stood in the middle of the street. A Guardia in a

brown khaki uniform lay motionless on the road not far from him. The Guardia's legs were crossed, his boots at a crazy angle to each other. A second Guardia knelt before Elías. The Guardia's rifle was on the road, an arm's length away. He extended an open hand imploringly toward Elías. Elías pointed his rifle almost casually at the Guardia's chest. Nicolás drew in a breath, and before he let it out Elías pulled the trigger.

The impact of the bullets lifted the Guardia up and then propelled him back. He came to earth in a heap. Except for raising two quick fingers to his mustache, Elías did not move.

Nicolás turned from the window and slumped back against the wall. "Virgencita," he said aloud. "Help me." He waited for the sound of more rifle fire. Where was Gerardo? Were there more Guardias out there? Choking down a sob, he again risked poking his head over the windowsill. He saw Elías pulling off the Guardia's boots. Nicolás left the schoolroom. As if walking upon slippery rocks, he made his way to Elías's side. "What are you doing?" Nicolás asked. He scanned the street and the broken-down buildings lining it. No more Guardias anywhere.

Elías grunted as he tugged at the second man's boots. "We're taking these. Also their backpacks and uniforms." Already Elías had slung the Guardias' rifles over his shoulder. "Pull that one's trousers off," he said to Nicolás. "Don't bother with his shirt. The bullets made a mess of it."

"Where's Gerardo?" Nicolás asked. He could not even contemplate doing what Elías had ordered.

"Back there." Elías jerked his head in the direction of Emilio's place. "These two here killed him."

• • •

Once again a human mule, Nicolás strained under four backpacks, a rifle, two pairs of boots, and his own machete.
Tucked under his arm was a sooty jagged blade, all that was
left of Emilio Sánchez's saw. Slung over Elías's shoulder, like
a human backpack, was Gerardo's body. The great wound
in his chest had spilled blood that had run down Elías's shirt
and soaked the fabric of his trousers. As if this were not
burden enough, two M-16 rifles hung down from Elías's
other shoulder. Yet he seldom paused for rest during the
two-hour trip. Nicolás trailed behind him, trying to draw
strength from Elías's grit. With the fierce sun beating down,
Nicolás kept his eyes on Gerardo's broad back, on the neat
curious holes that pocked his polyester shirt. He thought of
Gerardo's mother in her humble room outside Tejutla: La
niña Tencha, going about her business, oblivious to the fact
that her little king was gone.

seventeen

They buried Gerardo under the trees behind the rancho. He had Samuel for company when they laid him in his grave. With him, they buried the blatant irony that his death occurred on a mission to save the life of his grave mate, for in the end, retrieving Emilio Sánchez's saw was an act performed in vain. While the three were in El Retorno, Samuel's wounded leg had dispatched a blood clot to a lung, and neither Felix nor Eddy could do anything to save him.

After the burial, Nicolás became more taciturn than usual, and he was ready to cry at any moment. Now, two days later, he meandered to the river and traipsed along the bank until he reached the spot where the river veered toward the waterfalls. Because it was April, with the rains still two months off, the river was low and the cascades meek. Nicolás peeled off his boots and socks, and fully dressed, he waded out to his favorite rock. It was flat and broad. He rested upon it, his back curved to the water sheeting over him. He focused on the stream's sound, trying to erase the image of the Guardia that kept flooding his head. But he could not, try as he might. He saw the Guardia's hand raised beseechingly to Elías. He pictured Elías squeezing his trigger in response.

The rushing water pummeled him pleasantly, soothing his body and his mind. The falling water sprayed around him, and sunlight pierced the spray and magnified it with many-hued rays. Virgen Santa, he thought, because the light dancing about him was like the light sparkling down from her sainted hands. What am I to do? What am I to do when there is death all around me? As his mouth filled with water, he gurgled the words to her, listening for an answer, knowing that her voice could penetrate through the deep density of his despair. But there was only the sound of the splashing water.

His jeans were soaked through and through, and he could feel the weight of the denim building up against his thighs and calves. His shirt was thin, and plastered to him like a second skin. He looked downriver, catching the sight of water roiling there but then smoothing out farther down. If he were asked to express it, he would not find the words, but what he wanted for his life was this same kind of transformation. Simply put, he longed for still waters.

He sat like that for a time, sucking on the medal of la Virgen Milagrosa that hung from the chain around his neck. He thought about Gerardo and his mother and how one day he would knock on her door and hand her the hank of hair he had snipped from Gerardo's head with the Swiss army knife's scissors. He would tell her that, despite his affiliations, her son had been a good man where he was concerned. Nicolás watched the river flow past the trees and scraggle lining the banks motionless and without cheer in the brunt of the sun. He tried mouthing a prayer, but a prayer would not come. Presently, a little tune his mother used to sing came into his mind. O María, my Mother. My consolation. My protection and guide toward the heavenly realm.

He was picking his way up the riverbank when he heard Mario calling. "Nico! Nico!" What now? Nicolás thought, but increased his pace, because there was an ominous edge to the little boy's voice.

As he rounded a clump of brush, Mario ambushed him with a gleeful little jump. "There you are!" he said. "Come quick! It's Lidia. Lidia's pooping out a baby!"

• • •

Lidia was indeed having a baby. She was spread out in one of the lean-tos, and most of Dolóres's people, all the women, a few of the men, were there to witness it. Mario elbowed his way to the front to join the cook's little girls sitting cross-legged on the ground as if it were a picture show they were attending. Nicolás hung back with the men. Neither doctor was among them, tending, as they were, the wounded and ailing. Tata and Capitán were away fishing, so they would miss the spectacle.

And a spectacle it was. Nicolás beheld Lidia both squatting and leaning against Elías, who sat on a chair and cradled her in the width of his opened legs. Elías! It was Elías sitting there! Lidia's skirt was hiked up above her big round belly. She wore her laced-up boots, and her legs were spread to show a startling darkness between them. Nicolás watched in amazement. He watched Lidia's sweaty face, the way it contorted and grew red and then the way she let out a bursting exhalation and opened her eyes so wide they seemed in danger of popping out of their sockets. He watched her take in a long breath and scrunch her features up again, her eyes turning to slits, her mouth opened to an endless high grunt.

Rosario knelt before Lidia barking out directions. "Push! Push!" Rosario's little gold teeth underscored each command.

Push? Why push? Nicolás thought, and then he saw it: the wet black crown of a head emerging like the rounded wet head of a chick popping out from an eggshell. He took in a breath, widened his own eyes, and watched the baby slip out into the world as if it had been greased.

Rosario caught the slick long package in her ample hands. "It's a boy!" she exclaimed. Looking up to Elías, she added, "You got yourself a boy."

On the regular radio, a merry song played and brought smiles to the watchers. Lidia allowed herself to crumple. Elías stood up proudly. He lifted the chair away to give his woman room to lie back.

eighteen

That night, los guerrilleros celebrated. They held a party deep under the trees where the enemy would least look for the glow of the campfire. The people toted suitable rocks to sit upon and carried the rope cots out from under the gallery so the recovering wounded could join in: Chema, who needed cheering and who was now free from IVs, and three others who would soon rise from the cots and take up the fight again. Tonight they would enjoy an unusual feast. Chico, in charge of logistics, had trapped five wild rabbits and Carmen had made a succulent stew of them. There were stacks and stacks of tortillas and pots of beans and coffee. But the main treat was the cans of sardines harvested from the dead Guardias' backpacks. That and packs of filtered cigarettes, a large plastic bag bulging with fresh coffee beans, two smaller ones sparkling with refined sugar. "Ah," Carmen said when Elías brought the stash into the kitchen, "the enemy lives differently than us." That she was talking about their own native brothers hung unsaid between them.

Tonight they celebrated the birth of Noé, named after the biblical ark builder, and they honored the lives and valiant deaths of Gerardo and Samuel. So, too, they were taking their leave of Dr. Eddy, who tomorrow would move on to a medical surgery center in Arcatao. Only Victor, who had caught post duty at the riverbank, was not enjoying the camaraderie. To compensate, he received two sardine fillets instead of one. Were he a smoking man they would have upped his allotment of that treat as well. Orlando, the guerrillero who was keeping watch on the hill, was practically a participant since his post periodically brought him close to the party.

Nicolás wore his T-shirt with the big red bull on the front. Earlier, when Mario caught sight of the animal's flaring nostrils, he said, "Uy, mad bull!" and Nicolás placed his index fingers up beside his head for horns and stamped his feet and charged. Mario had yelped and then broken into a laugh. Now, however, Nicolás was in a somber mood, subdued by the realization that, in a span of a few days, he had experienced life at its extremes: an end and a beginning. In so short a time, would the pendulum of his life ever swing as wide? The salty taste of one sardine had also quieted him. Though he had wrapped the fish in a tortilla and washed it down with gulps of coffee, its oiliness remained at the back of his throat, and he could not fathom what the fuss was about where sardines were concerned. He sat quietly on a log and took everything in: the frogs in concert down by the river, the crickets under the trees, chiming in with their own chorus. The bright spit of burning wood. Its smoky odor. The dark canopy of trees that draped like Our Lady's mantle over them.

After dinner, most of the men, with the exception of Tata, who was not feeling well, were smoking cigarettes. Some of the women were, too. Carmen, for one. She inhaled

great drags and then exhaled long plumes with great satisfaction. Nicolás sat across from her, and in the fireglow, he
thought her nostrils looked like the nostrils of the bull em-
blazoned on his T-shirt. Dolóres, the boss, also had a cigarette, but as she spoke to them, she waved it in her hand
more often than she puffed on it. When it burned down, she
dropped it to her toes and ground it out with her boot. "Will
you look at this," she said, raking her foot back and forth
across the ground. "This land is nothing but silt and rocks.
It's good for nothing but stumbles. There's no topsoil here.
No nutrients. You want to know why? I'll tell you why." In
colonial times, she explained, the land had provided indigo
and its blue dye to European weavers and English textile
factories. Their very own ancestors had worked the añil, she
said. It was famous on the world market for its vibrancy and
purity. The ancestors had endured the greed of hacienda
owners, who, in an effort to maximize profits, overworked
the tribes and overtaxed the land: indigo was grown year
after year and was not rotated with other crops such as
beans and corn. This abuse of the land caused deforestation
and severe erosion. At the turn of the century, and perhaps
as a just reward, Germany manufactured a synthetic dye
made from coal, and thus the añil industry was laid to rest
forever.

She gave a grunt of disgust. "It's no wonder we have
come to revolution. Our great revolution is made of many
smaller ones. Each of us sitting here is an act of revolution."
Her M-16 was propped between her legs and rested against
her thigh. "Now look at this," she said, holding up the rifle.
"Half of us here are without one of these." She turned and
nodded in the direction of Elías. "But thanks to our comrades, two more arms came our way."

"Long live my man," Lidia said. She cradled her baby, and now she lifted him in the same fashion as Dolóres had when she hoisted up the rifle. "Long live the revolution. May it live long for my Noé."

Dolóres nodded. "That's right. Gerardo and Samuel, they died for Noé. Think of that. Think of the truth in that when the food runs out, when our ammunition runs out, when it's only machetes we have. When it's only hatred we have to fuel us." She paused for a moment and then went on. "Use your heads, comrades, use your heads. Revolution. It means turning around. We are turning our lives around, the lives of all the people."

Her pronouncement silenced them all for a moment, and then Chema spoke up, which was a good thing, given that for days he had lain on his rope bed and hardly a word had come from him. "When I first joined up, all I had for a weapon was a stick and a hemp sack. That's all. I used to drape the sack over the stick and pray it looked like I was hiding a rifle."

"All I had was my machete," another man said.

"Well, I had that, too," Chema said. He lay propped against a rolled-up straw mat. He was wearing a shirt, for the nights were always cool, but it was unbuttoned, and the incision down his abdomen looked like the tracks laid down for a train. "We've all had them. Through the years, we've always had our machetes."

"Something sharp and with an edge," Eddy said.

"Well, it's time to catch up with something explosive," Felix added.

"For decades, the enemy has relied upon experience," Dolóres said. "He's had decades to train and fortify and grow. Compared to the enemy, we're in our infancy."

"We're like Noé." Lidia looked down upon the innocent face of her son.

"We're like Noé now," Elías added, "but growing stronger and more hardened every day."

Dolóres said, "Let's not forget Che's saying, 'To grow hardened, yes; to lose our tenderness, never.' "

Carmen mashed her cigarette with her flip-flop. She stood and tossed her head. "Speaking of tenderness, how about a little music? This is a party, isn't it?" As an inducement, she gave her shoulders a little shake.

Dolóres said, "Good idea. Where's the guitar?"

Soon, Elías played and the people sang softly. Despite the dire circumstances, they thanked life for giving them so much. They sang about overcoming. They sang about triumph and victory. When all their melodies were spent, they took turns around the fire and told each other things.

Enrique told about the day he got shot in the butt. "For a long time it wasn't easy to take a crap. I used to hold it in because it hurt so much."

"Too bad you couldn't hold that wind of yours in," Joaquin said, because he had been with Enrique when Enrique was hit. Dodging fire, he had scooped Enrique up off the trail where he had landed. He had thrown Enrique over his shoulder like a gunnysack. Carried him all the way to the field hospital in Arcatao.

"A man has to relieve himself any way he can," Enrique said.

"My relief came when you stopped all that farting," Joaquin said, and everyone laughed.

"It was the beans," Enrique added lamely.

Carmen said, "Everybody blames beans."

Eddy said, "In the United States, we have a little song

about beans. The song says, 'Frijoles, frijoles, la fruta musical.' " He went on and regaled them with the whole of it, doing a little jig around the fire while everybody clapped to keep rhythm with him.

When their laughter died down, Carmen said, "So let's have beans for every meal. That's funny, seeing how most times beans are all we have anyway."

"I ate a snake once," Lidia said.

"We roasted it over a fire," Elías explained. "We were on a forced march, fleeing from the town where we lived. The enemy came and bombed us out. Set fire to all the houses. Burned our fields and the corn and beans that were ready to be harvested. We'd been on the march for three days without a thing to eat when we stumbled upon a boa constrictor. The serpent was so big it laid entirely across the road. We chopped off its head. Made a small fire under some trees. Roasted him up."

"When you're hungry, snake's pretty good," Lidia said. She had lifted up the bottom edge of her blouse and Noé suckled her dark nipple.

"Does snake taste like garrobo?" Chema asked. Lizards were a common source of food in the markets.

"No," Lidia said. "Garrobo tastes like chicken." This comment brought the heartiest laughs, given that the people rarely had chicken on their menus.

When the fire turned to embers, when stories and the ribbing died down, the people doused the coals and picked up their rifles and machetes and backpacks. Sleepily, they retired to their resting places.

Tata and Nicolás did not speak as they climbed the hill on their way to the cave. The moon hovered large and bright, and so there was no need for the beam of the flashlight.

When they had squirmed past the opening in the rock, Nicolás lit the votive next to his little statue. On an impulse, he lifted the statue down and laid his lips against the tiny rent on Our Lady's cheek. He set her back on the ledge again before turning to his grandfather. "Tonight Dolóres said we are an act of revolution. Am I an act of revolution, Tata? Are you?"

Across the cave, the candlelight projected a bulky image of his grandfather up against the wall. "No, my son, you are not an act of revolution. We are not."

"Then what are we, Tata?"

"We are caught in the middle. That's what we are."

nineteen

A week later, around mid-morning, Norberto, one of the guerrilleros who had gone out on a reconnaissance trip, ran breathlessly into camp with bad news. An informant who had just returned to his hamlet from Chalatenango told him of an army directive ordering a number of units to conduct clean sweeps. He had, he said between gasps, seen one of these units not far from the rancho. He took a deep breath, holding his side, describing what he had observed. About a dozen men, all armed with assault rifles and one with a portable communications pack strapped to his back. If they found the camp and radioed in the location, Norberto said, an air strike would surely follow.

Dolóres threw back her shoulders and clapped her hands. "Vacation time's up. We've been here three weeks. Had to happen sometime." She gave the order, and within minutes the whole of the camp was like a swarm of worker ants retreating from a fire line.

Nicolás lent his hands to the massive effort. Tata, though feeling poorly, also pitched in. He had slept fitfully the night before due to a pounding headache. Today, in the heat, sweat slipped from his brow and dripped upon the firebombs he and Nicolás were nesting in two Styrofoam chests.

"Are we going with them?" Nicolás asked. Dolóres had pointed out that if they stayed behind, the army would consider them sympathizers. "No matter what we take away," she said, "from the looks of the place, it's pretty obvious we've been here." She had motioned toward the stacks of cut bamboo and felled tree branches lying beside the lean-tos they had erected when they arrived. She had indicated the heap of trash that had accumulated over time next to the cooking shed.

"We're not going anywhere," Tata answered Nicolás. "This is our home. We'll hide in the cave." Because they were made from glass soda bottles, the firebombs tinkled when he laid them one upon the other. "Go over to the kitchen," he added, raising a shoulder and using it to dry his dripping chin. "See that Carmen doesn't pack up our cooking things. Also, see if you can separate her from some of that food she was making for lunch." In the copinol, a few birds chirped cheerily. Capitán hauled himself up from a snooze under the tree. He stood as if rooted there and looked from group to bustling group, bewildered.

Nicolás checked on Carmen in the cooking shed. She was ready to dump out the frijoles that had been simmering in a pot. That pot she would take with her. The tortillas she had made, she was stacking in a basket. "That pot's ours," Nicolás said, pointing out another one. "Put the beans in there." He rescued their coffeepot. Their frying pan. The long-handled spoon that for years had rested inside the bean pot.

"Aren't you going with us?" Carmen asked. "You can't stay behind."

"We're staying in the cave," Nicolás said. "Can you part with some tortillas?"

She shook her head ruefully; still, as if they were playing cards, she stacked ten tortillas. "There," she said, handing them over. "You should go with us, Chelito."

"Gracias," Nicolás said, partly in thanks for the tortillas, partly because she cared enough to not want him to stay.

Within the hour, the people were marching off toward the west, toward a more mountainous and pine-covered region. They had packed up the cumbersome radios and the batteries. They had lashed the generator to a pole for two men to carry. They had dumped medical and kitchen supplies into cardboard boxes. They had piled provisions into rush baskets to be balanced on their heads. The remaining vials of medication and plastic cards of whole blood filled two of the Styrofoam chests. Every shoulder, arm, and neck became an extension for something to hang on: a backpack, a rifle, the guitar, the awkward light sockets with their coiled-up extension cords. For the first time in two weeks, Chema left his rope bed. With help from Rosario, he had climbed into a hammock, his awaiting ambulance. Thankfully, the other wounded had risen from their recovery beds and pronounced themselves fit enough to march.

The people did not stop to say good-bye. One by one they went off, most carrying what seemed to be more than their own weight. They did not apologize for commandeering Blanca, who was needed for milk, and the speckled hen for her eggs. Tata and Nicolás stood in the middle of the yard, watching as the forest cut the last of them from their view: Lidia with Noé strapped like a pack to her back. Little Mario, holding on to his mother's hand, looking over his shoulder, his bottom lip atremble. As he disappeared under the trees, Nicolás turned away, and his gaze fell upon the doorway to what, in another life it seemed, had been his room. The table Felix had used for surgery was framed by the opening. Spread over the table was Rosario's sheet with the faded cabbage roses. To Nicolás, those little roses were the saddest sight in the world.

• • •

Tata and Nicolás secured themselves in the cave. They hauled in water and filled the pottery jug to the brim. They brought in the fishing gear, the pot of beans, the stack of tortillas. They dragged leafy tree branches in through the tunnel, stuffing them in the chinks between the big rock and the mouth of the cave. This camouflage plunged them into darkness, so they used the flashlight to light their way back down the tunnel, where they piled up branches at the exit. Capitán was with them, and after all had been done and only waiting remained, Tata tied the dog to Blanca's chain lest he try to stray. "Vaya, vaya," Tata murmured reassuringly. He rubbed circles between the dog's ears before he tied a leather thong around its snout as a guard against its barking. Capitán gave a shake or two and pawed the encumbrance, but Tata patted his big head and the scruff of fur down his back, and soon the dog quieted down.

"You can turn the flashlight off now," he said to Nicolás. They sat side by side, the dog sprawled between them, on squares of flattened cardboard, like flying carpet squares, their machetes resting in their laps. In Nicolás's pocket was his Swiss army knife. Wrapped around it, two one-colón bills. They sat with their backs against the wall that rose at a right angle to the tunnel. If the cave were penetrated from the river side, an intruder would have to step past them, allowing plenty of time for a machete to hurl down.

Nicolás switched off the flashlight but kept his hand on it. The blackness that enveloped them was so complete that he had to blink his eyes to make sure he had not disappeared. "Are you there, Tata?" he felt compelled to ask.

"I'm here," his grandfather replied. He laid a calming hand on the boy.

"Are you scared?" Nicolás wished for the votive to be flickering in the niche, but they could not risk even the tiniest light that might give them away.

"Don't be afraid. We're safe in our cave."

"Your hand is hot, Tata. Did you know your hand is hot?"

"We did a lot of work just now. It made me hot and caused me to sweat."

"Oh." The answer satisfied Nicolás, who had been anxious because, earlier, he had noticed the sweat pouring off Tata's brow, but more than that, the way he laid his fingers against his temples, as he himself had done when the sickness had come and he had thought his head might explode. In their small space, the odor of beans and tortillas was magnified, and though he was not hungry, he decided to concentrate on this. After a moment, and almost to himself, Nicolás whispered, "We'll be all right."

"We'll be all right," Tata repeated.

Less than half an hour later, about noon, a growl began to rumble in Capitán's throat.

twenty

Ninety-some minutes after the people fled, a dozen soldiers approached the rancho, keeping to the trees and fanning out in a semicircle around it. The sun was high, and though its light breached the vegetation, it lost most of its brightness on the way and only dappled the ground. As the soldiers reconnoitered, they noticed the remains of a campfire, the ring of rocks around it, the cigarette stubs peppering the trampled soil. The men inched forward into the clearing. They did not speak except through hand signals. One soldier nudged over an empty sardine can with the tip of his boot. They noted abandoned lean-tos, five rope beds sitting in a row under a jerry-rigged gallery. Beyond this stood the rancho itself. A red-tiled shack abutted it. Next to the shack, a mound of trash. The whole of the place was unnaturally serene, but they did not rely upon surface appearances. The leader, a tall, thick man, motioned to the two soldiers flanking him. With little steps, they softly trotted toward opposite sides of the hut, sidled up along the gallery, and looked back to their leader, who made a nonchalant throwing motion with his hand.

The grenade fell upon a table draped by a sheet. For only

an instant, the grenade balanced there, like a strange pocked fruit, and then it rolled off. When it blew, the concussion shattered the table, embedding slivers of wood into the bahareque walls, compressing, then expanding them outward. The soldiers had hit the ground, but when the boom produced by the grenade died away, when the flying bahareque and the palm fronds from the roof ceased to be missiles in themselves, the men clambered up and sprinted into the room, their rifles drawn and firing.

In the cave, the grenade's report was heard as a dull, hollow bump. The rifle fire that ensued—-the unmistakable metallic ripple of automatics—caused Capitán to jerk up on all fours. In the dark, he lunged, straining against the chain that held him, striking his big head against the jug that held the water supply. The jug tipped over.

Nicolás felt the wetness spreading over the cardboard they sat upon and he, too, jumped up. "¡Tata, el agua!" he exclaimed, remembering to keep his voice low. Now that his eyes had adjusted to the dark, he could see Capitán tugging on the chain for his freedom. Pawing at the leather thong that kept his muzzle shut, he growled and whined. Tata stood and stumbled, then struggled to right himself, as if he had been sleeping and risen too quickly. He took hold of the chain and pulled the dog down. "Vaya, vaya," Tata said to quiet him. He squatted beside the dog, spread one hand over its head, and raised the other to his throbbing temple. Nicolás set the jug upright. He lifted the cardboard squares and let the water roll off. It was too dark to see it, but he knew that the thirsty cave bottom had already soaked up the moisture. He placed the squares aside and hooked an arm around the scruff of the dog's neck. "Quiet, Capitán, quiet."

Outside, half the rancho had been blown away, but the

adjoining cooking shed remained upright. The grenade and rifle volleys had produced no hideaways, so the remainder of the squad advanced into the yard, shouting invectives.

"Oh, listen," Nicolás whispered to his grandfather. Beyond the big rock, and dangerously close, came shouts and threats: "Assholes! Sons of bitches! We're going to blow you away!" The threats shrank the cave's protection into something unsubstantial and perilous.

Nicolás's ears were ringing with fear. He held Capitán down, but the dog's hide squiggled under Nicolás's hand. "They'll find us, Tata."

"Shhh, shhh," Tata said, one hand on the dog's muzzle, the other on his own pounding head.

Once certain the place was abandoned, the soldiers regrouped in the yard.

"They were here, all right," one of them said.

"We must have just missed them," another said, jerking a thumb toward the shack, where embers still smoked in the fire ring.

"They can't be too far away," the leader said. "Get the captain on the radio."

The man who carried the radio walked over to the nearest lean-to, swung the apparatus off his back, and set it up on a table. He checked the calibration and made contact. "Ready, Lieutenant."

The lieutenant stepped over and took hold of the phone. "Teniente Galindo here, mí Capitán. My men and I are on a hill, about a two-hour hike north from El Retorno. We found a deserted guerrilla camp. Looks like they had a field hospital of sorts. There's rope cots and plenty of used medical supplies in the trash. They can't be very far if they're transporting wounded. An hour or two at most. It might be worth a look by helicopter." The lieutenant gave the location's coordinates to the captain.

Soon enough, the ugly thump of a helicopter rotor sent the birds flying from the trees. Galindo heard it before it rose up past the hill and appeared over the trees. It hovered for a moment over the rancho and then hooked a wide swoop to the west. Minutes later the far-off sound of machine guns erupted. Long rhythmic bursts of fire. Quiet. Long bursts again. Then a thunderous explosion. Then another. Like the finale of a giant fireworks display.

• • •

Galindo and his men headed west, following radio instructions from the captain: "The copter caught up with the guerrilleros. A number of them are down. Others scattered in the hills. Take your people up there. Tell me what you find."

twenty-one

What they found was carnage. Seven dead, among them a woman and an infant strapped to her back, a man wrapped in a hammock like a netted brown trout, and two men, no doubt the ones transporting him. There was a woman with the top of her head blown off and with her mouth gaping open. Two of her front teeth were gold and these glinted in the sun. The seventh body was unrecognizable. What was clear was that whoever it was had been carrying explosives. This was confirmed by a Styrofoam chest filled with homemade firebombs found up the path that had survived the air attack. The bodies were lying close to one another, but an odd mix of things littered a much wider area: tortillas tucked into the grooves of a generator, sugar sprinkled like fairy dust over bulky communication batteries. A disposable latex glove rested like a milky hand upon a box lashed with hairy-looking cord. In addition to the bodies, a gruesome enough sight, blood was splattered on pots and pans and provisions. A bag of tortilla flour lay split upon the path. Blood painted a pink trail through it.

Lieutenant Galindo sent his sergeant and two men down

the trail ahead, a path no wider than an ox cart. He posted four others above and below the trail as a precaution against a counterattack. That left five to scour the immediate area for more dead or wounded and to pick through the debris. Two others had caught the easiest duty: they had stayed at the camp in case any guerrillas doubled back.

"What a mess," Galindo muttered, turning a circle on his heel.

"Why all this blood so far away from bodies?" one of the soldiers asked.

"Looks like they were carrying plasma," another soldier—this one a sergeant—said. He picked up a plastic bag bulging with rusty liquid. He held it for an instant, its corner pinched between two fingers, then he let it drop. He stomped on the bag with the heel of his boot, but the plastic did not break.

They rifled the pockets of the dead searching for information, but came up empty. Then they set about destroying equipment and supplies that had remained intact after the air strike. Where it proved effective, they used the firebombs to do it. They shot up the generator and the batteries, using as little precious ammunition as needed to get the job done. The sergeant used the butt of his rifle to knock out the two glinting gold teeth from the dead woman's mouth. They broke away easily with one sharp, well-directed tap. He slipped them into his pocket, wiping them against the leg of his uniform first. A soldier with a bulldog's mashed-in face salvaged a guitar. When they had a little time back in Tejutla, he said, he would regale them with a song.

Disappointingly, no rifles nor other arms were found. These they would have bothered to transport. "The bastards probably only had thirty-thirties," the sergeant said, for there was a popular guerrilla song extolling the virtue of joining the rebellion with such an antique firearm.

Mission accomplished, the lieutenant rounded up his men. They radioed the captain at the garrison with the news. He ordered them back to the rancho for the night. "In the morning, come back to Tejutla," he said.

The lieutenant lifted an arm as a signal for them to leave. He figured they would reach the rancho just about nightfall. As they started down the incline, a small boy materialized from around a boulder. The boy was calling for his mother. He held a rifle in his hand.

• • •

To Nicolás it seemed that the last time he had taken a breath was just before the helicopter had roared overhead. Now all was quiet. His heart had stilled and he could breathe again. Capitán had settled down. Tata had been sitting with his back against the wall, but some time ago he had slumped down, and now he was curled like an infant, each big hand bunched against a temple. Nicolás laid a palm against Tata's forehead. "You have a fever," he said.

"My head's exploding."

"Do your bones feel like they're breaking?"

"Yes."

"When I was sick, I felt like that." What Nicolás did not say was how anxious he was that Tata's fever might reach the height that his had reached, that the fever would burn him up and he would die, curled up like that in a cave that was growing darker and more stifling by the minute. Nicolás reached into the jug and discovered there were still a few scoops of water left. He scraped some up with the tin can that served as a ladle and bade his grandfather have a drink.

Later, when darkness came and night was an ally, Nicolás would go down the tunnel and steal his way to the river for more.

"Gracias, hijo," Tata said, and slurped the water. He lay down again, his hands against his head.

Nicolás went across to the niche that held his statue. He brought her back to where he had been sitting. He set her on his lap, encircling her with his arms so that she rested against his heart. He wanted to say a prayer. His mother had taught him to pray when afraid, but the only words he could think of were the same old words he always said: Holy Mary, Mother of God.

He sat like that, totally inert, his head against the wall, looking out into blackness. Fiercely he wished for something but could not even name something to properly wish for. Then an astonishing thing occurred: before he could question it, a thought burst into his mind and tumbled from his mouth. "I am a lion in a cave," he said to himself. As if it were a litany, he felt compelled to repeat the words, and as he did, the statue grew warm against his circling arms. Soon, it grew warm against his chest, too. He lifted la Virgen up. In the gloom, he inspected her as best he could, but there was nothing different about her, only the increasing warmth she emitted, as if the rays of light he had seen spill from her hands were locked inside her today.

Soothed by her warmth, Nicolás fell asleep. Some time later, he could not guess how long, the racket made by the frogs on the river awakened him. It was pitch-black now in the cave. He could feel the weight of the statue against his lap. He laid a hand on her, but she was no longer warm. He raised her up and pressed her against his heart, feeling his grandfather's presence in the dark. "Tata, are you awake?"

Nicolás spoke just loud enough to be heard above the serenading frogs.

"I was thirsty so I had a little water. There's still some left if you want some."

"No, gracias." He wasn't hungry. He wasn't thirsty. "Is it almost morning?" Nicolás asked because Tata could tell time just by the way the frogs sounded.

"Not yet."

"Do you think the soldiers are gone out there?"

"Maybe."

"Do you feel better, Tata?"

"I'm better."

"You know what? I dreamed about la Virgen. I dreamed her statue was very hot and that it warmed my heart." He said it was a dream, but he knew that it was not.

"That was a good dream you had."

Nicolás nodded. "You know what else? I dreamed about a lion. I dreamed I was a lion in a cave." It was Our Lady who had sent the words into his mouth. He knew that, too.

"Another good dream. Lions are brave and they are strong. You are a brave and strong boy."

Nicolás smiled, pleased that his grandfather thought so well of him.

"Go back to sleep," Tata said. "Soon enough, morning will come."

• • •

Nicolás opened his eyes to a crease of gray light showing between the big rock and the cave mouth. Outside, birds warbled their wake-up songs. He sat up and cleaned the corners of his eyes. He made out the figure of Tata lying on his side, next to Capitán. Both snored softly in tandem. The statue had slipped away from him, and Nicolás felt around the floor until he found it. As he placed her back in the niche, his hand stumbled upon the little wooden lion Basilio Fermín had carved. Astonished at the coincidence, Nicolás slipped the lion into his pocket next to his Swiss army knife. He thought, I am a lion in a cave. I am brave and strong. He needed the words, the talisman itself, to give him courage to do the thing he had to do. Before it got too light, he would go down the tunnel, slip past the tangle of camouflage, and make his way to the river for more water. He picked up his machete and Tata's turquoise fishing bucket. As he proceeded, he repeated the litany in his head: I am brave. I am strong. I am like a lion. Soy valiente. Soy fuerte. Soy como el león. Each word buoyed and lifted him.

He had filled the bucket when he realized he needed to relieve himself. He stepped away from the river, leaving the bucket sitting in the water. There was a bush nearby and he set his knife down, unzipped himself, and squatted and did his business. He stripped a clump of leaves from the bush and wiped himself.

He was fastening his belt when he felt the poke of the rifle barrel against the small of his back. "Well, look what we have here," someone said.

twenty-two

The corporal prodded Nicolás with an M-16 up the path toward the rancho. Nicolás kept his arms above his head. He could not believe that, once again, and almost on the very spot, calamity had befallen him. His pulse raced. His scalp tightened around his skull. When he stepped into the yard, he saw that the rancho was in ruins. Where once had been a roof under which he had slept, there now was but the dim outline of the hill in back, a sketch of trees, a smudge of sky. Nicolás turned his head away from the devastation, from the odor of his past rising up from it. He thought of Tata waking up in the cave. Tata finding him gone. Tata coming out to look for him.

"Look what I found, mí teniente," the corporal said as he drove Nicolás toward the center of the yard. Toward the group of soldiers standing there.

"Where was he?" the lieutenant asked.

"Down by the river."

"Who are you?" the lieutenant demanded. "What's your name?"

Nicolás's mind whirred. For an instant he thought of

taking an alibi in the tradition of the guerrillas, but the effort of such a dodge was overwhelming. He decided on the truth. The truth with certain limits. "Nicolás de la Virgen Veras, mí teniente." He used the title the soldier had used. For added courage, he spoke Our Lady's name.

"Where are you from?"

"From here. This is my home." With hands still above his head, Nicolás pointed a finger toward the rancho.

"Where's your family?"

So soon had they arrived at the place where truth needed trimming, where caution and furtiveness were imperative in the telling. "Until the guerrillas came, it was just me and my grandfather who lived here in the rancho, Teniente." Nicolás held his breath against the repercussion this bold information might have. He was thankful there was not enough daylight to fully shine on his expression. That the lieutenant's expression, too, was being kept from him. To be safe, Nicolás wiped from his mind the image of Tata sleeping in the safety of their cave.

"So you admit that the guerrillas were here."

"Sí, Teniente. They built lean-tos and made rope cots for their wounded. A few weeks ago they came over the hill and took over our rancho. My grandfather and I, we had no choice." He noted how easily he could tell the truth. That it did not cause him a moment's hesitation.

"Mmm . . ." the lieutenant said, clearly mulling over the admission. "Where's your grandfather now?"

Virgen Santa, Nicolás thought. I am brave. I am strong. I am like a lion. He needed the whole of Our Lady's power to clear this hurdle lying before him. "The guerrillas took him, mí teniente. They took me too, but I got away."

"When was this?"

"Yesterday. La capitán Dolóres heard over the short-wave that the army was coming. She gave the order to leave. She said my grandfather and I had to go, though we wanted to stay."

"¿La capitán Dolóres?"

Nicolás nodded. "She was the boss."

"What happened when you left? Which way did you go?"

"We went that way." Nicolás turned toward the direction where he had seen the last of the people vanish under the trees. His arms ached from the exertion of keeping them aloft. He lowered them slowly and propped them on his head. "My grandfather was helping to carry a hammock with one of the wounded. When the helicopter came and started shooting, I ran into the trees, but my grandfather lagged behind. You see, Teniente, my grandfather is old."

"When did the helicopter come? When was that?"

Nicolás thought, This is a test and all is lost if I don't pass it. "In the afternoon when the sun was not so high. I ran into the trees and down to the river. I could hear the shooting; I even heard explosions." He prayed he was not asked further about this detail, having heard the sound of what he thought were explosions while hiding in the cave. He prayed he was not asked why he had not returned to the spot of the assault after it was over. What would he say if the officer posed that?

"Explosions?" the lieutenant asked. "What explosions?"

Nicolás lifted his shoulders. "I don't know. I think maybe the helicopter crashed." Not knowing the cause, it was all he could think to say. To veer from the perilous topic, he added, "Last night I hid in the brush, then followed the riverbank back to the rancho. I thought my grand-father would be here by now. I'm going to wait until he comes."

The sergeant said, "I don't think your grandfather will be appearing any time soon."

"We're going to Tejutla. The kid's coming with us." The lieutenant turned on his heel.

"Or I could blow him into the next world so he wouldn't be a bother," the sergeant added.

El teniente swung back to face the sergeant. "Isn't the one you blew away yesterday enough for you, Molina?"

Molina lifted a hand in a salute. "I beg your pardon, mi teniente."

"The kid has information. We will bring him to the captain for questioning."

The lieutenant paused for a moment, then he gave an order: "Torch what's left of this junk heap."

Nicolás dropped his hands to his sides at the sight of his rancho going up in a whoosh of flame. All his treasures the fire consumed before his eyes: the two rooms that had contained both his life and his dreams. The shed, darkened by the soot of so many cooking fires. Even the copinol tree under which he'd sat to rest, to hone his machete, to scratch Capitán behind the ears. When the leaves of the tree trembled and curled into themselves, he groaned and, heedlessly, dashed to it and pulled away the bench that for years had abided there. He had been sitting on this bench when his mother came striding toward him with the gift of new boots. On the bench when she had calmed his fears about la Ziguanaba. Now, he dropped the bench on the ground before the soldiers. For a moment, he did not care if they did as the sergeant had threatened. He would welcome being blown into another world. Into a place where his rancho was forever nestled against the hillside. Where Tata snoozed peacefully in his hammock. Where his mother and he sat in the shade, her arm thrown around him, her laughter a happy tune in his ears.

twenty-three

They brought him to Tejutla. To the army garrison in the center of town. When they arrived, the lieutenant marched Nicolás through the wide front doors (they were thrown open during the day, but guarded on both sides by soldiers), down a short entry hall, and around to the left to the captain's office.

The lieutenant saluted his superior. "Look what we found up in the mountains, mí capitán. The boy was with the guerrillas. Perhaps he knows some things."

Alert and wary, Nicolás stood before the officer who was a wall of hard flesh rising like a rampart behind his desk. His neck was so wide it disappeared into his shoulders, shoulders upon which were pinned two gold bars. In a sweeping glance, Nicolás took in the whole of the room: the file cabinets, the tables stacked with papers, a communications radio and its confounding dials, a black oscillating fan. On the wall was a big framed photograph of the president of El Salvador.

"What's your name?" the captain asked.

"Nicolás de la Virgen Veras, Capitán."

"And how old are you, Nicolás?"

"I am nine years old. In June, I will be ten."

"What were you doing up in the mountains?"

"I live there with my grandfather." He went on to repeat the story he had previously told. As he spoke, Nicolás was conscious of the lieutenant, still at the door behind him, and so he doled the information out carefully, making sure he left nothing out. Making sure he added nothing.

"Tell me about the guerrillas," the captain said. Behind his desk and over to the side, a window spanned by iron bars opened onto the street. From where he stood, Nicolás could see the intersection. He could spot the Esso oil drums forming a barricade from sidewalk to sidewalk. He could see the back of the soldier standing post at the corner. The crossed straps of his bandolier. The canvas pouches hooked to his belt and bulging at his sides. He could see the M-16 hanging at his shoulder. The dull-looking dome of his helmet.

"Like I said, a few weeks ago they came over the hill and took over our rancho."

"How many?"

Though he was weary to the bone, Nicolás squared his shoulders because this was his moment. He must win this man over with proper information. "There were thirty of them, Capitán. Twenty men and ten women. The boss was called Dolóres. They also called her capitán."

"What kind of a weapon did she have?"

"It was called an M-16."

"What about the others?"

"M-16s too. Maybe eight of them. And they had a short-wave, but not as good as what you have." Nicolás jutted his chin in the radio's direction. "They had a generator for electricity. They used the electricity to light up the room when the doctor did the surgery."

"A doctor did surgery?"

"Yes. He was named Felix. He operated on three people, but one of the people died. His leg was blown apart and it was hard to keep the flies off. There were even worms in the leg."

The captain gave a little wave, a dismissive gesture. "What about explosives?"

"They made firebombs." Nicolás stopped there, lest he picture too vividly Tata sitting under the lean-to smelling of match heads, lest what he pictured in his head the officers might also see.

"What kind of firebombs?"

"The kind made with bottles and candles and matches and gas."

"Molotovs," the captain said.

Nicolás said nothing because the word was unfamiliar, but he went on for a bit. "They built lean-tos and rope cots for the wounded. They had classes for studying the alphabet. They spent a lot of time looking at big maps."

"What about the shortwave? Did they get instructions and information over it?"

"The radio had a lot of static, Capitán. They talked over it, but I couldn't understand what they said."

For a moment the captain was silent, then he asked, "What else did they do?"

"Most of the time they rested."

"Rested?"

"Yes. The captain Dolóres said it was their vacation."

At this both of the officers laughed, then the captain said, "And what about you? Was it a vacation for you?"

"No, Capitán. I had to haul water. Pails and pails of it up from the river. I helped the cook in the cooking shed. Her name was Carmen. I also helped with the wounded. Sometimes I had to stand by the rope cots and shoo away the flies with a square of straw mat. Back and forth over the wounds. The wounds were ugly, Capitán. They didn't smell very good. Especially the one with the worms crawling out."

The captain waved his hand again, then he switched the topic and fired off two questions. "Where's your mother? What's your grandfather's name?"

He was standing at the edge of a cliff, and had he not been prepared, the questions might have pushed him over. But he was ready for them. On the trip to Tejutla he had replayed in his head the story he would tell. He spoke it now: "My grandfather is Don Tino Veras. He's old; he's sixty-six. All his life he's lived on the rancho. All my life I've lived with him. My mother died when I was born, and ever since then it's been just Tata and me, living at the rancho, growing our corn and beans, our millet down by the river. Until the guerrillas came, our life was tranquil. Then they came over the hill and changed everything. The guerrillas took my grandfather away." Nicolás dropped his head. He didn't have to work at feigning sadness. Just mentioning his mother, his grandfather, caused his shoulders to droop. It sent tears brimming. "I need go to back to the rancho, Capitán. I need to wait there until my Tata returns."

As if wanting a longer view, the captain leaned back in his chair. "I don't think that's a good idea. And let me tell you what else. I think you're a valiant boy to stand here before me confessing what you've been through. You say you and your grandfather spent time with the guerrillas. You say it was by force. That they came over the hill and took over your place. Well, that's something that's open to question. I myself am pretty certain about things. I'm certain that any-time citizens consort with the guerrillas, it's a voluntary thing. This grandfather of yours, this Tino Veras, you can be sure that if he survived the helicopter strike we ordered late yesterday, the man's up in the hills. Old or not, a guerrillero's a guerrillero. This grandfather of yours, he won't be returning to your rancho. Trust me on that. If he survived, he and the rest of his comrades have taken to the hills. After our assault, they'll be laying low. They'll be tending their wounded, because, believe me, after that strike of ours, that doctor Felix you mentioned will have plenty to do. That's if he even made it through the strike. Do you understand what I'm saying?"

Nicolás nodded; what he was hearing sent a whirlwind through his head. An air strike. People dead. People wounded. The captain thinking Tata was a guerrillero. Nicolás had to keep reminding himself that Tata was alive. Tata was not a guerrillero. Tata was in their cave.

"Now that brings us to you." The captain drew himself against the desk again. He thrust the barrel of his chest upon it. "It is a certain fact that even kids like you can be guerrilleros. How else can it be when it's family and friends consorting and abetting the guerrillas? What kind of example is that? I tell you what kind. It's a very bad example, that's what it is." The captain leaned back again. "Okay. So now you're here with us and you might be asking yourself, 'What will they do with me?' A very good question." The captain smiled a fleeting smile. "Well, Nicolás de la Virgen Veras, this is your lucky day. You might not think so, but it is. Why? Because today, I'm feeling generous. Because today, I'm feeling sorry for a boy who's been living a bad example. As such, I'm going to see that you get a new chance." He smiled again; this time his upper lip stretched flat against his teeth. "To do it, we're going to keep you here and turn your life around. Here with us, you'll be shown a different example. Isn't that right, Teniente Galindo?"

At the door, the lieutenant said, "Sí, mí capitán."

The captain went on. "You probably don't know this, and despite anything to the contrary you might have heard, the National Army is about discipline and about order and about obedience. It's about offering its members a different kind of life. Do you understand what I'm saying?"

Nicolás nodded again.

The captain pulled himself forward and narrowed his eyes. "But let me tell you something else about the army. The army won't tolerate subversives and informers and anarchists. It won't tolerate malcontents with militant ideas. It won't tolerate idealists and dreamers and reformers whose mission it is to change the world. The army is sure and swift when it comes to rabble-rousers. I'll spare you the gruesome details, Nicolás de la Virgen Veras. Pay close attention to what I tell you: we are giving you this chance to improve your sorry life. We catch you talking with anyone suspicious; we catch you scheming or trying to get away; the whole of the National Army will fall on you like buzzards on rotting meat. The scene won't be pretty. It won't be pretty for you or for anyone we catch you consorting with. Do I make myself clear? Do you understand what I'm saying?"

"Sí, Capitán." What he understood was that he was free-falling off that cliff after all.

To nail down the fact, the captain addressed the lieutenant, "See that he gets fed. Get him cleaned up. Then put him to work."

Leaving the office, Nicolás made a resolution. He would escape from here as soon as he could. How he would accomplish this, he did not know. Of one thing he was certain: he

was capable of whatever it took to do it. He was a lion, was
he not?

• • •

While the soldiers had their meal in the dining room off the
patio, Nicolás ate at a table in the kitchen where Ofelia was
the cook and the supreme commander of whomever entered
her domain. She was a tall, skinny woman as old as Tata,
Nicolás guessed. She had salt-and-pepper hair caught in a
knot at the nape of her neck. She strode imperially in and
out of the kitchen brandishing platters of fried syrupy plan-
tains, rice folded through with black beans, little yellow
squashes filled with cheese, chunks of beef in a savory sauce.
She ordered Silvia, the young woman who cleaned and
helped with the serving, to pay more attention to the food
and less to a certain soldier, the one named Vidal, the one
they called "el Chucho" because he had a mashed-in nose,
like a bulldog's. All the while she worked, Ofelia maintained
a running conversation with whomever she had in front of
her, adjusting the subject as necessary. When it was Nicolás's
turn to receive her attention, she spoke to him as if she had
known him all her life. "Eat that meat. It'll put some flesh
on that scrawny body of yours."

Nicolás made no response to the comment; all the words
he had to say had been said already. He could not remember
a day when he had spoken so much. In fact, he was exhausted from so much talking. From so much explaining and
trying to keep his wits about him. Still, he was not too tired
to do Ofelia's bidding. Everything on his plate was delicious
and a revelation. When had he had more than tortillas,
beans, and rice, maybe a hunk of cheese, an egg fried up in
lard? When had it ever been more than a little chicken for a

treat? Here, even Ofelia's tortillas were thicker, more flavorful. He loaded a wedge of one with meat and was transporting it to his mouth when she saw him do it. She stopped in her tracks, marched over, and picked up the fork she had laid down next to his plate. "This is a fork," she said, poking it into his hand. "You're in the army now. Use it." She went around the table, then added, "When you finish with that, we're turning you over to Chabela."

Ofelia went out into the dining room, leaving her statement to hang in the air. When she burst back through the door, she continued. "Chabela's going to wash those clothes you have on. Do you realize how dirty they are?" She wrinkled up her nose. "How long has it been since you've had a proper scrubbing?" Out she went again, leaving Nicolás in suspended animation. What did she mean, he needed a scrubbing?

Nicolás bent his head over his plate again. He speared his meat and took a bite, the metal of the fork feeling foreign in his mouth. Not that this was the first time he had used a fork. He wasn't a savage. It was just that it wasn't customary. He had his hands for eating, did he not? It occurred to him that if his clothes were to be washed, he would have to take them off, and this realization caused him no small amount of anxiety. What was he going to wear while his clothes were being washed? Certainly they didn't want him standing somewhere naked, did they? Thinking of his clothes caused him to remember the items he was carrying in his pocket: the two colón bills, the little wooden lion, the Swiss army knife. He placed a hand on them, his anxiety taking a leap. In no way could he let them know that he owned these things. Especially the knife. He would have to hide them. And he had to do it quickly, before this person named Chabela got hold of him.

• • •

Late that night, after he had stashed the contents of his pocket on the ledge under the kitchen table; after Chabela had surprisingly handed Nicolás a fresh set of clothing (they were her son's, she said) and he had experienced the novelty of bathing under a showerhead; after his duties had been assigned and described; after the garrison doors had been drawn and shuttered and the soldiers had bedded down, all thirty-some of them in rows of cots; after the lights had been doused and the only sound was that of men snoring, of the back-and-forth bootfalls of the two guards outside; Nicolás lay on a petate, next to the open barracks door. He had been offered a cot, but he did not want one. Though he was as weary as he had ever been, he could not sleep.

Ten years before, the garrison had been a family home, a sprawling, one-story place with a large patio and a wrap-around tiled corridor as its focus. Back then, the patio, surrounded by high walls, had contained a water fountain, rosebushes and gardenias, an umbrella tree, a mango tree, and an ironwood. The flowers had lent grace and perfume to the air. Canaries, housed in slender-reed cages that hung from the trees, had brightened the mornings with song. When the army took over the house these amenities were sacrificed for military practicality: a bare quadrangle for flag raising, roll call, and calisthenics. Because it gave both fruit and shade, only the mango remained. In the army, usefulness was a saving grace.

Nicolás looked out the door, past the darkly gleaming corridor and out into the patio. The lamp on the street corner threw its light over the walls and onto the tree and the two German shepherds lying under it. The dogs were named Principe and Princesa. He could not tell them apart; they

were robust black dogs ticked through with pale fur and
ruffs around their necks. After the evening meal, when the
soldiers had been on the corridor cleaning their rifles, Nicolás had sat at the patio edge, observing the men and the dogs.
Noting the layout of the place. He had sat nearly motionless,
so as not to be noticed, permitting the dogs to come up and
to sniff him.

Now he slid himself and the thin mat, a little at a time,
out the door and over the width of the corridor. He needed
his mother, his grandfather. The thought of them, so far
from him and unreachable, was like a knife thrust in his
chest. Slowly he advanced toward the tree and the familiar
consolation of warm fur. The dogs watched him come, their
ears pricked, their eyes alert. As he proceeded, he kept close
to the ground so as not to overwhelm them. As he crept
along, he murmured reassurances: "Vaya, vaya." Just like
Tata would have done.

twenty-four

Since his arrival a week before, each time Nicolás awakened to the trumpet blare at reveille or lined up with the soldiers for roll call; each time he was made to do push-ups or jumping-jacks alongside them, or he raised a hand to salute the officers, or bent his head over their boots as he applied a spit-polished shine; each time these things happened, his grandfather's face filled Nicolás's mind, and it was as if his Tata were calling him home. When this happened, Nicolás pictured the blackboard at school and how la señora Menjivar would ask him to use the powdery eraser and wipe the slate clean. He did the same with Tata's face, with his mother's, looming there like ghosts in his head. Better not to focus on separation and homesickness. Better to concentrate on how he might escape.

Today Nicolás worked in the kitchen with Ofelia. Later he would go with her to the market and help carry back the baskets of provisions. After that he would mop the corridor, sweep the front and back sidewalks, and hose them down clean. A mere week had gone by, and already his duties were numerous. His compliance and cooperation were demanded and expected. In the army, there was no such luxury as time to adjust.

"I don't see why you choose to sleep with the dogs," Ofelia was saying to Nicolás. For days she had been stuck on the same subject. She had appointed herself to be everybody's mother; she was the kind of woman who did not need an invitation to dole out advice. She was at the stove sautéing chopped onions and tomatoes in a frying pan. The vegetables hissed and sputtered in the lard she had spooned in and smelled delicious to him.

"I like dogs," Nicolás replied by way of defense. He went into the pantry to scoop a pan of black beans from the sack on the shelf. He pulled a string and the light went on. The place smelled of bean dust and corn. Open shelving rose against the walls and held kitchen tools and supplies. From there he could still hear Ofelia going on about the dogs. "Dogs are dogs," he could hear her say.

Nicolás hefted the bean sack from the shelf and placed it carefully on the floor. He unfolded the top and thrust the pan inside, sinking it deep, hearing the satisfying sound the beans made as they rolled into the pan. Once the pan was filled, he set it aside. He was returning the sack to its place when he noticed something peculiar at the back of the shelf. Where the wall rose up, there appeared to be a long shadow, like a slash. Nicolás set the sack on the floor again. He reached across the shelf and touched the wall, feeling a protrusion, like a seam. He stepped back and looked higher. The seam climbed the wall. He could see it here and there behind the items on the shelves. A few inches from the ceiling, it turned and continued horizontally for a meter or so, and then descended again. I know what that is, he said to himself. That's the outline of a doorway.

"What are you doing?" Ofelia said from the kitchen. "Did you fall into the bean sack?"

Nicolás hastily finished up in the pantry. He saw Ofelia at the stove, blowing a strand of damp hair off her forehead. "As I was saying," she went on. "You're a boy. A boy shouldn't sleep with dogs."

Nicolás shrugged, because he didn't know how to respond to a comment like that. He sat on a stool at the kitchen table and sorted through the beans, picking out the dirt and pebbles. He raised the medal of la Virgen Milagrosa dangling from his neck chain and sucked on it. The medal was the only thing from home he risked letting others see. He believed Our Lady was keeping it safe from confiscation. The little carved lion, the Swiss army knife, and his money he had restashed in a knothole in the mango tree. He had discovered the hiding place after the dogs had allowed him a space beside them. And so, yes, so what if he were sleeping with the dogs? The dogs protected and comforted him.

The fascinating novelty of his surroundings could not free him from the trial he endured. Not the place itself with its shiny tile floors and thick adobe walls, not the myriad rooms for sleeping and eating, not even the two rooms for doing your business and for cleaning up. Not the coziness of the kitchen, nor the wonder of the contraption with the iron rings on top needing only a key to be turned for the wavering flame to shoot up and be of service. Not even the refrigerator taking up the space against the wall, an appliance as impressive as the one he had seen in el señor Alvarado's lilac-colored house. When Nicolás and the soldiers had marched into town, they had passed his house. It was only two blocks from the garrison. The sight of it, and not far from that, the sight of la Farmacia El Buen Pastor with the painting of Jesús and the lambs above the lintel, the sight of the post office on the corner, the very place from which his mother's letter had departed, all these things added to his disconsolation and made more fervent his desire to escape. But there he sat, on the stool in Ofelia's kitchen, his face a stone, his mind wielding and brushing away any thoughts that could betray him.

"Listen to that," Ofelia said, nodding in the direction of the noise coming from across the courtyard. "Who can cook with that going on?" She looked over her shoulder to the door. "Will you shut that, Nicolás?"

Nicolás went to the door. He looked down the corridor toward the room next to the office that served as an interrogation room. It was from there that the commotion came. Shouts, whacks, groans, the sounds of someone gasping for air. This morning a group of soldiers on patrol had brought in a man suspected of subversive activities. The man was dirty and bedraggled. He wore no shoes. His thumbs were lashed together behind his back with a length of henequén twine. For over an hour the man had stood in the office before the desk of Captain Portillo. Nicolás had been mopping the corridor, and each time he passed the door he cast a quick glance inside. Each time his eyes fell upon the self-same thing: the man's two big thumbs growing thicker and more purple by the minute. The captain's questions frightened him: "What is your name? Where do you come from? Who funds your activities? Who are your comrades? Name them, or else!"

Nicolás closed the door. He resumed his chore of picking through the beans.

After a moment, he said, "What do you think will happen to him?"

Ofelia had moved the frying pan off the flame. The tomatoes and onions were limp and had given up all their juice. She was at the table now, breaking the ends off the green beans. "Who knows," she said.

Neither spoke for a while, both lost in the sounds of muffled moans, the sharp snaps of the beans, the tumble of frijoles being sorted in the bowl. "One thing I do know," Ofelia said at length. "If I were that man, I'd tell them everything."

twenty-five

He had dreamed about escaping, and she had spoken to him again. Last night, la Virgen Milagrosa had appeared in the dream. They had been in the pantry, which was small like a cave. She was resting on the shelf, as she had in her niche. The rays emanating from her hands had backlit the wall, illuminating the seams of the plastered-over doorway. Above the top seam and on the wall itself, the saying ENTER HERE appeared. In the dream, Nicolás sounded the words out: "Ehn-treh-ah-quee." The very impact of the message had awakened him. He lay there, under the mango tree, his heart beating fast. Our Lady had spoken again. She had shown him the way.

Now it was up to him to determine what lay on the other side of the door, what he would be stepping into when he broke through. Such sleuthing would not be easy. Inside the garrison, there was rarely an opportunity to explore. He had his duties, and every hour was occupied. In addition, he feared the eyes of the captain and the lieutenant, each capable of popping up at any place at any time. Outside, twenty-four hours a day, a soldier patrolled each street corner. During the day, a pair stood guard beside the front and back doors. All were armed. All of them took note of him each time he appeared. They watched him while he swept the corridor and hosed off the sidewalk. While he polished the boots, they watched him. While he was in the kitchen, Ofelia did too. So did Silvia, when he helped her set out the serving dishes in the dining room. And in the market, the cook never let him out of her sight. He studied Ofelia sometimes, studied her placid, grandmotherly face, and he felt the sorry need to crawl into her lap and burble out his story. But when this ache arose, he felt the electric thrill of caution jangling inside him, and he thought: She might not be a soldier, but still, she works for them.

This morning, Nicolás stood on the front sidewalk, hosing it down. Across the street, the sun was just poking over the tops of the buildings: the eating place, its tables crowded already with people; the shoemaker; the funeral parlor, called El Porvenir—What Is to Come. These last two places had yet to open, but an employee from each was diligently sweeping their sections of the sidewalk with a wide rush broom. The brooms swished rhythmically as they swept. Nicolás moved the black rubber hose up and down. He liked the feel of it in his hands, the way a continuous stream of water flowed out its end. A miracle really, when compared with lugging pails up from the river at home. Nicolás hooked a thumb over the hose's end and reconfigured the water's delivery: now a thick spurt, now a fine mist that sparkled and made a splendid rainbow in the sun. He had taken off his boots and socks, preferring the feel of the warming sidewalk against his soles. Sometimes the water felt like something other than water, something silky, like a cloak. At home, the Sumpul River felt that way sometimes. Especially down by the cascade, when he was alone, sitting on the flat rock mulling things over.

Nicolás reached the corner where Vidal was posted. Vidal was called "el Chucho," the Mutt, because of his mashed-in face, but Nicolás never addressed him that way. He called him Señor Oficial, as he did all the soldiers. Every night, as Nicolás lay under the mango tree, he observed Vidal leaving the barracks and making his way down the corridor to the latrine. Then he and the dogs watched him shuffle back to his cot again. This morning, Nicolás nodded to him as he stood on the corner. Lucky for him, Vidal's post placed him in front of la niña Rocío's store, so an icy Coca-Cola was always a possibility when the sun parched his throat. The store was the only business to share a space on the block with the garrison. When the army moved in, they decided the store's location was providential: the men had only to walk a few steps to avail themselves of cigarettes and action comics and glossy girlie magazines. The store was good for morale.

Nicolás tugged the hose to a new stretch of sidewalk. The splashing water turned the new patch as dark as wet river stones. The sound of metal clanging caught his attention. He looked across the street, toward the middle of the adjoining block, to the poster store. The owner had thrown open the two metal doors. She hooked giant-sized images of Rocky, the movie prizefighter, and Raquel Welch, the siren, to the top of one door. On the second, she displayed images of Jesús and Saint Joseph. That's much better, Nicolás thought.

The front sidewalk cleaned to perfection, Nicolás walked past the soldiers at the door and traversed the short hallway that led to the patio. He turned the spigot handle and shut off the water. He hauled in the hose, yanking and pulling until it was bunched in the middle of the patio. From the spigot, he had a good view of the garrison and of the soldiers

congregating in the dining room and finishing breakfast.
Their rifles rested in the floor racks, their heads bent over
their plates. Ofelia and Silvia carried platters of fried eggs
and casamiento, the "marriage" of black beans and rice,
around the table. In all his life, Nicolás had never seen so
much food, had never eaten such hearty fare. He turned from
the sight and opened the spigot again, pulling the hose under
the tree and past the wide opening that separated the main
patio from the back one. Here labored Chabela, usually
arched over the washbasin, rolling a yellow ball of soap over
yet another soldier's uniform. Nicolás raised a hand in greet-
ing. At the moment, she was leaning against the kitchen
doorway having herself a smoke, the only other activity that
occupied her time. "Nicolás," she said, smoke curling up
from her thrust-out bottom lip.

He kept his thumb over the hose's opening, diminishing
the stream of the water as he pulled the hose around the
captain's jeep, down the short driveway, and past the broad
doors that opened onto the back street. The sun stood higher
now, and it shone brightly on the walls of the businesses
across the street. Near the corner, a solider was positioning
one of three Esso oil drums across the pavement to form a
barricade. During the day, the troops stopped all traffic in
front and in back of the garrison, and checked all driver
identifications. Nicolás dropped the hose and trotted over to
give the soldier a hand. The oil drum was empty but cumbersome to manage. After they had wrested it into place, the
soldier turned his back to Nicolás and moved down the
street.

Looking back up the street, Nicolás saw the guard there
also had his back to him. Nicolás thrilled with the realization
that, if he sprinted now, he could make it around the corner

before the soldiers turned around. He had stepped up on the sidewalk when a simple reality stopped him. He was not wearing his boots. He could not escape without his boots. He stepped back into the street just as the soldier near this corner pivoted to face him. Nicolás sauntered innocently toward him. "Let me help you with the other barrel," he said. On the sidewalk, the unattended hose spewed a steady stream of water. Above it, the glass shards embedded at the top of the patio walls glinted in the sun.

• • •

For lunch, her hands and mouth never idle, Ofelia made chicken soup rich with vegetables while Nicolás sat at the kitchen table. She reminded him of Doña Tencha, the mother of Gerardo (may he rest in peace). When he got out of here, Nicolás thought, when this nightmare was over, he would retrieve the lock of Gerardo's hair that he had saved in the letter box in the cave. When times were safe, he would take Tata with him and present himself at Doña Tencha's door. Lay his offering of remembrance in her tired motherly hands. The thought of this saddened him, as did the thought of his lost opportunity. He chided himself for thinking that being barefoot would make a difference. He should have run anyway. Rocky, rooty terrain or not, he could have made it home without his boots. Hadn't Tata spent his entire life without the encumbrance of boots? To distract himself from such negative thinking, Nicolás half listened to Ofelia, who was rambling on about tomorrow. Tomorrow was the third of May, the Day of the Cross. She wanted Nicolás to build her a cross. The one they used last year had not stood up to the festivities. After lunch, she wanted Nicolás to forage in the shed out by Chabela's washbasin. Find two good pieces of lumber. Nail them together into a good sturdy cross. Nicolás nodded periodically, intercutting the gesture with either a "Sí," or a "No." While she lectured on, he thought about the pantry. He pictured his escape route embedded in the wall. If he took his Swiss army knife to the plaster there, he might be able to carve away at it, if it were crumbly enough. It would take time, of course, and he would have to work at night, while the others slept. The dogs would not give him away. It was only Vidal and his nightly round-trip to the latrine that he would have to watch out for.

"Did you hear what I was saying?" Ofelia asked, her voice rising like the steam from his soup.

Nicolás looked up. Smiled. Nodded. Said, "Sí." What was she talking about?

"I said, when you get the cross done, we'll go to the market. I want to get fruit to decorate it. Let's see. I want paternas and mangos, cocos, guineos, coyoles, and granadillas. Do you like granadillas?" she asked.

Nicolás smiled again. Shook his head. Said, "No."

"You don't?"

"Sí."

Ofelia batted a hand. "These kids," she said, and huffed out the door.

He blew on his soup. He lifted the bowl and slurped it from the rim. Before he knew it, she walked back in like a gust of unexpected wind. "I saw that!" she exclaimed. "In the army, we use spoons!"

He raised the spoon in a salute to show her he would comply.

• • •

Chabela the laundress was mute compared to Ofelia, a trait Nicolás appreciated. She matched his inclination to say as little as possible at all times. He was in the back patio, nailing two wide planks of wood together for Ofelia's cross, while Chabela leaned over the washbasin, her hand sweeping back and forth over somebody's uniform. The ball of soap she used made a smooth rolling sound. It had an antiseptic odor that Nicolás found not at all unpleasant. Chabela had already scrubbed and soaped a half dozen shirts. Draped over the bushes growing along the wall, they were bleaching in the sun. If he narrowed his eyes and used his imagination, the bushes looked to Nicolás like plump soldiers dressed in uniform.

"What do you think?" Nicolás said, lifting the cross up and holding it at arm's length for her to see. The cross was as tall as he.

"It's better than last year's," Chabela said. Back and forth, back and forth her arm glided. "By the way, sometime today I want to wash those clothes of yours. You can wear something of my boy's while I do."

He looked down at his T-shirt, the one with the charging bull on the front. He remembered little Mario. The time he, Nicolás, had pressed his hands beside his head to make horns and scraped a foot along the ground like an angry bull. "¡Uy!" little Mario had said, his eyes big with skeptic amusement. "What's your boy's name?" Nicolás asked Chabela.

"Gustavo."

"How old is he?"

"He's ten."

"Do you live with him?"

Chabela stopped scrubbing. She turned to look at him. "Of course I live with him. Why?" Nicolás shrugged. He returned his attention to the cross. Gave the nails holding the two beams together a couple of good whacks with the hammer. Before he knew it, she was beside him, her arms hanging at her sides and dripping water. Before he could say anything, she had laid an arm around him. Pulled him to her so that he smelled the soap on her and the odor of honest labor. "You're like a little lost lamb." She gave him a quick squeeze before loosening her grip.

He gulped down the knot in his throat, hoisted the cross, and laid its transecting beam over his shoulder. "Where do you think Ofelia wants it?"

"Over by your tree." Not moving from the spot, Chablela watched the boy going across the patio, bearing his burden. She wiped her hands on her apron. Then went back to the washbasin. Picked up the soap. Rolled it back and forth across another shirt.

Squinting back tears, Nicolás dragged the cross into the front patio and stationed it against the mango.

The garrison was still quiet. Half the soldiers were away on a sweep. They had risen earlier than usual and had out-fitted themselves with heavy weapons from the armory. Nicolás tried not to pay too much attention to what they said or where they might be going. He did not know what he would do if he learned they were going to El Retorno.

"What you doing with that?" The voice of Vidal, sitting out on the corridor, taking a break after lunch, surprised Nicolás. Vidal motioned him over, then nodded toward the cross when Nicolás drew near. "What you going to do with that?"

"Tomorrow's the Day of the Cross."

"So it is," Vidal said. "My mother loved to decorate the cross. She set it up in the yard. Made paper chains and draped them all over. Mounded flowers and fruit all around it. I used to snitch the fruit, but Mamá would come running out of the house with the broom, 'That's for the cross,' she'd yell, and bat at the air. I'd go flying in the other direction, a long paterna under my arm. Paternas were my favorite. How about you? Did your mother do that?"

Nicolás looked down at his boots. At la niña Flor's, was his mother setting fruit around the base of a cross? Were la niña Flor's daughters helping with the decorations?

"Where you from?" Vidal asked.

Nicolás lifted his head and looked at him. What purpose was there to these questions? Was the man just being friendly, or was this the start of some kind of interrogation? "I'm from up in the hills," he said circumspectly.

"Dangerous place, the hills," Vidal said.

"Did you get a Coca-Cola?" Nicolás replied as a way to divert the conversation.

"A Coca-Cola?"

"When you were standing post on the corner, in front of the little store. Did la niña Rocío give you a Coca-Cola?"

"Oh, that. Yes, she did. I like Coca's, don't you?"

Nicolás nodded. He thought of Vidal trudging to the latrine each night. Wondered what Vidal would think if he knew that, on almost every trip, he was being watched.

"Speaking of the store," Vidal said. "I want you to run over there. I need a pack of cigarettes. Embajadores, they should be." He leaned back and straightened out a leg. Dug into his pocket and extracted a colón. "Here. Go do it now. And keep ten cents for yourself. Buy yourself some caramels. Or if you want, a Coca-Cola."

Nicolás took the bill and went on the errand. Down the corridor, around the corner, down the entry hall. He lifted the bill to the soldier posted at the door. "El Oficial Vidal wants something from the store," he said. Nicolás felt the burn of the soldier's eyes all the way to its door.

La niña Rocío sat on a high stool behind a glass case

filled with merchandise. She was a woman of who-knew-what age, discreet, and of good cheer. She had a plump body draped in a flowery fabric. Her radio was on, tuned to a station playing a ballad about someone having a bed made of stone. La niña Rocío was mouthing the words and swaying a little to the music.

"A pack of Embajadores," Nicolás said, laying the bill on the counter.

"The cigarettes. They are for you?" She kept a straight face when she said this.

"No. They're for the soldier Vidal," Nicolás said.

The store owner used her hand to push against her face. "Ay, sí. The one with the face like a bulldog."

Nicolás smiled but said no more. He watched her give a little jump from the stool. Heard her grunt when her feet hit the ground. "Embajadores are my most popular cigarette," she said. "I just ran out of the loose packs I keep in the vitrina." She pulled the stool over by a unit of open shelving set against the wall. "Could you climb up there, Chelito? I keep the cigarette cartons stacked up on top. Get a couple of them down for me, will you."

For a moment, the fact that she had called him Chelito, that familiar nickname of his, disconcerted him, but he went around the glass case as told, climbed on the stool, and reached for what she needed. The store was poorly lighted, and when he had come in, he'd had to wait for a moment before his eyes adjusted. But now, standing on the stool, he could see around the items stored on the shelves. He could see sections of the wall. A seam climbing it. He reached for the cigarette cartons, and before he picked them up, he reached farther back and let his fingers rest for a moment on the seam. He felt a soft, plastering-over. Just like in the pantry.

twenty-six

The pantry and the little store shared a common wall. This he now knew. He imagined Our Lady writing EXIT HERE over the shelving in the store, just as he had dreamed she had written ENTER HERE in the pantry. Since his discovery a few days before, he had taken the blade of his Swiss army knife to a section of wall. He discovered it was made of wooden laths mudded over with plaster. Because the wall had replaced a doorway and appeared to have been hastily erected, the plaster was scant and soft and crumbly. The laths were narrow and flimsy. Once they were exposed, a few swift kicks would knock them loose.

He decided he would work on a section that was low and not easily noticed. He would forge an opening as wide as his shoulders and wiggle through on his belly. To do it, he would use the short crowbar he had found while rummaging for wood in the patio shed. He would take his time so as not to give himself away. When the opening was ready, he would make his getaway while the soldiers slept; while la niña Rocío was safely tucked in her bed at home. Once in the store, he would wait to hear the receding steps of the soldier on the corner before turning back the lock on the door, pressing it open just enough to get past, closing it back softly. Already, he savored the feeling of freedom that would come as he dashed across the street.

This morning, as he wiped down the tables in the dining room, Sergeant Molina, the one with the nappy hair, the one who had been up at the rancho with the others, called out to him. "I've got a job for you," the sergeant said. "We're going to target practice, and I want you to carry some of the ammunition." What Molina really meant was that he wanted Nicolás to carry *all* the ammunition. All thirty-five pounds of it.

Nicolás followed Molina down an interior hallway to the armory door. Until this moment, whenever Nicolás had passed the place the door was always padlocked. This morning it was thrown open; inside, el teniente Galindo was pulling down ammunition boxes from a shelf and stacking them on the floor. When he saw Nicolás, he lifted the hinged lid from one of the metal containers and pointed to the clips with the rounds inside, nestled against each other like zipper tracks. "Put twelve clips in there," he ordered, pointing to a backpack lying by the door. Nicolás did as he was told; he focused on his assignment but remained keenly aware of the weapons and supplies that surrounded him. Years later, when he had a full understanding of such things, he would describe in detail the rows of M-16 assault rifles resting at an angle in the floor racks, the Colt.45 automatic pistols suspended against the wall in their own holders. He would recall the stacked boxes of NR-20-CI hand grenades. The half dozen rifle grenades with launchers. The containers of rifle and pistol ammunition. He would tell about the dynamite and the blasting caps, about the ancient Mauser rifles, the old Thompson submachine guns. The Browning M-2s and the Stoner 63 with its tripod mounting, ugly and awe-some in the corner.

He transferred the long clips into the pack, each clip loaded with thirty shells. As he stacked them, they made that peculiar click of metal striking metal. He cinched the pack shut and hoisted the straps over his shoulders. The weight hung against his back, and he had to stoop a bit to adjust to it. He had been here two weeks, and in that time he had not toted anything as heavy. He left the room and waited just outside until the lieutenant had padlocked the door.

A dozen soldiers were scheduled for target practice. They had congregated in the corridor, waiting for Galindo and Molina, who were the range officers of the day. Vidal was one of the soldiers. He strode up to Nicolás. "Looks like you're the pack mule today."

Nicolás shrugged. He wanted to say something like, I'm always the pack mule. He wanted to say that, as such, he was a good pack mule, and tell about the time he had hauled an ice chest filled with whole-blood packs clear up the mountain to his home. He liked this man Vidal, if for no other reason than Vidal seemed like a human being, not just a soldier with mayhem on his mind. Three nights ago, after Ofelia had decorated the cross in the patio, after dinner and before lights-out, Vidal had brought a guitar to the corridor. He reminisced about his mother again and how she loved the ritual of fruit and flowers and the cross. He strummed a song about homesickness. He had a mellow voice, and he sang low and sweetly about being far from the place where he was born. He sang, "An immense nostalgia invades my thoughts." Because it was a song, the words seemed right, and no one in the garrison had mocked him for voicing them.

"One good thing about that," Vidal said, pointing to the

backpack. "You'll be lugging it full to the rifle range, but
it'll be empty on your way back." He showed a happy,
toothy smile, which seemed to flatten his nose even more
against his face.

The rifle range was not far—three blocks east and then
four blocks north—but to Nicolás the trip seemed intermi-
nable. The straps of the pack dug into his shoulders, and his
legs ached with the strain of so much weight. He walked
beside the lieutenant, doubling his pace to keep up. He could
not stop for a rest or to reposition the load; he could only
focus on the steady tromp-tromp-tromp of the soldiers who,
led by the sergeant, marched importantly down the center of
the streets, causing pedestrians and traffic to either stop or
proceed slowly around them. Sweat soaked Nicolás's T-shirt,
which he had tucked into his jeans because the captain in-
sisted on tidiness for everything. The group passed a cantina
pulsating with blaring music. In the middle of the next block,
they passed the house with the lilac walls. Then the pharmacy with the image of the Good Shepherd and his flock
above the lintel. Finally, the post office where his mother's
letter had begun its magical journey to her heart. All these
reference points gave Nicolás courage, for all had been proof
that once he had been another boy, that once he had lived
another life. A life he was determined to reclaim.

• • •

A high barbed-wire fence surrounded the rifle range. A padlocked gate kept out those who had no business there. A
wooden sign posted on the gate shouted a warning to those
who could read it: MILITARY RESERVE. THE NATIONAL ARMY
OF EL SALVADOR. ENTRANCE PROHIBITED. A deep ravine devoid of vegetation cut across the range. Lieutenant Galindo

stood under the only source of shade, a length of corrugated tin spread over poles, his eyes covered by dark, mirrored glasses, a clipboard under his arm, a pair of field glasses jutting at an angle from his chest. Galindo kept an eagle eye on the six soldiers lined up on this side of the embankment. The men aimed their rifles toward targets on the opposing side, one hundred meters away. The paper targets, the size of a three-foot-wide window, were circles set inside circles, a big bull's-eye in the middle, and were attached to two-by-fours sunk deep into the ground.

Nicolás stood close to Galindo, half-in, half-out of the sun because he did not wish to overstep his bounds and steal too much of the officer's shade. Nicolás took mental photographs of everything. The way Sergeant Molina strode from one soldier to the next, chiding the men into the correct manner of snapping the clips into rifles. The way Molina rebuked them into assuming the right stance, into holding the rifles properly before they fired each round. Nicolás listened as the sergeant radioed the pit crew across the ravine that firing was to commence. He saw the men receive the message and then take cover in the trench that ran below the targets. He heard Galindo bark out "Fire!" Watched each soldier shoot a single round, the reports of their firing occurring almost in unison and ringing in Nicolás's ears. He watched the pit crew receive the "All clear!" message. Watched six men poke their heads out of the pit and raise their marker poles to the spots where bullets hit. He watched Galindo peer into his field glasses and study each target. What he observed, he transferred to his clipboard in bold, quick strokes. For complete misses, the pit crew waved a red flag, and on this side, the sergeant called out "¡Magi!" a bastardization of "Maggie's drawers," a term the army had learned from the gringos who had trained the officers at the Salvadoran military school.

Almost two hours later, the dozen soldiers had fired at the targets from standing and squatting and prone positions. Each had fired exactly thirty rounds—this precise keeping count a necessity given that ammunition was expensive (a colón a round) and scarce, and therefore not to be wasted. The final destination of each shot had been duly recorded by their lieutenant, who, based on the scoring, would assign each soldier a grade. In that time, the soldiers had emptied their canteens of fresh water. Their camouflage uniforms were soaked with sweat. In that time, Nicolás had studied every move the soldiers made. He knew that if he had to, he could do what they had done.

• • •

That night he lay curled under the mango tree, the dogs asleep beside him. Ofelia's cross stood three paces away. With considerable effort, he had sunk the end well into the ground and then packed in rocks around the base to secure it. By now, the flower chains the cook had made for decoration were limp, their colors faded. The fruit she had laid out for adornment smelled disturbingly overripe. Nicolás peered up at the moon shining through the mango's branches. It recalled la Virgen back home in her niche. The face of the statue had that same moon milkiness. He thought of la Virgen and heard again the strains of the "Ave María." He remembered the words Our Lady had given him, the warmth she had burned into his heart so that he would never forget: I am brave. I am strong. I am like a lion.

He repeated the words to himself, low and soft and like a lullaby: soy valiente, soy fuerte, soy como el león. One of the dogs was lying close, and he laid an arm around it, feeling its moist and easy breath. He missed Capitán. He missed the rancho and his Tata. He missed his mother. Thirty-eight days since he had seen her, since she had led him into the plaza for Monseñor's funeral. Thirty-five since he had said a prayer and handed his letter to her over for posting.

"Mamá," he whispered, as the truth, sheer as gossamer, drifted down from the milky face of the moon past the lace the tree leaves tatted and settled down on him like a mantle. His mother was gone.

The weight of the truth; the weight of all things crushed him, and he sat up and propped his back against the tree and gasped to catch his breath. His mother was dead. At the knowledge, a wild grief overtook him, and he stood to confront it, a hand against his mouth to stifle the deep sob mounting up from his chest. He would never see his mother again. This truth he could not face, and so turned from it. Walking swiftly but quietly, so as not to alarm the dogs and raise the soldiers, he transported his grief to the back patio. He circled the captain's jeep. He paced around it once, a second time, while his mother's face, her voice, the earthiness of her scent, whirled in his brain, confounding him. Despair lashed his heart, and he fell against the wide iron door, his shoulders against it, his mouth open in a mute lament. His knees turned weak and he slid slowly down until he rested on the ground. The tears came then, steady, hot, plentiful. His mother was gone. His mother was dead. He would never see his mother again.

twenty-seven

The old man sat beside the church under the forlorn remains of the conacaste, his back against the tree's split trunk, his legs drawn up to his chest, as he had for the many days he had waited for the boy. Since returning from San Salvador, he spent most of the time like this, his gaze on the dirt road transecting El Retorno. He did not want to miss, even for a moment, the sight of the boy appearing, like a mirage, coming from who-knew-where, rushing toward him to reclaim their life together. As the sun sought the horizon, the old man shook his dog awake, and the two shuffled into the tumbledown church to nap in the spot he had claimed along the one standing wall under Our Lady's niche. Her statue filled the space again, and he drew comfort from it. He had brought it down the hill with him on that terrible morning after he had emerged from the cave, still in the grips of a fever, to find the boy gone, to find his past reduced to ash.

If he lived as many years as he had already been granted, he would not forget the sight of the boy's machete cast away in the brush beyond the cave's mouth, his own turquoise fishing pail bobbing in the water. Even down at the riverside, the sharp odor of burning had reached him, and as he clambered up the path toward the hut, he had prepared himself to meet devastation and calamity.

Calamity he had also encountered on the trip to the capital. Arriving at la niña Flor's door, he found the boy had not come as he had hoped; he learned that Lety, his only child, was dead. They came just like that: two stunning announcements. Such grief could topple a man, and there were times, while hunkered beside the tree, when he thought he would be better off in the grave. But then he pictured the boy, the yellow-green hue of his eyes, his somber demeanor, and the old man knew he must be strong and have courage. As the boy himself had said, he must be like the lion.

He prayed that the boy was keeping his own counsel wherever he might be. The old man had speculated on what might have happened that morning when he lay feverish in the cave: Nicolás going out for water, Nicolás captured by the army, Nicolás taken to a garrison and questioned, beaten, or worse. These were dreadful possibilities, so the old man had pictured a more benign scene: Nicolás escaping and reuniting with his mother. When he learned this was not so, the old man had haunted the capital's bus station. When his vigil bore no fruit, he had returned to la niña Flor's, where Basilio Fermín, the chauffeur, had called various army garrisons in the hope that Nicolás had been brought there. But all the places called, including the garrison in Tejutla, denied having seen a slender boy with tea-colored eyes.

Heavyhearted, the old man returned home to again scour the area around the rancho. He trekked into the hills when the winds brought the smell of something dead, and found what remained of Dolóres's unit. He had pinched his nose against the stench, and held his breath against the awful chance that one of the bodies might be that of his grandson. But praise all the saints in heaven, this had not been so. And while the fact allayed his greatest fear, the truth was that the whereabouts of Nicolás were still a mystery.

A middle-aged woman with braids piled atop her head came into the street. She cupped her hands around her mouth and hollered, "Don Tino! Breakfast!" It was Ursula Granados, the tortilla maker. She had returned home a few weeks ago, as had a handful of others who had fled El Retorno after the attack. When the old man took up residence at the church, Ursula watched over him. It was the least she could do, she said. After all, Nico had stayed with her while attending school. He had been like a son to her.

"Vámos, Capitán," the old man said. He unfolded himself slowly and stood, poking the dog with a callused, horny foot to get him going. The dog was old, too, and the misery that had befallen them had slowed him down as well. The old man gave his hat a pat and picked up his machete and the boy's as well. Together, the two old companions ambled down the street toward Ursula's.

As he wished, Ursula had set his breakfast in the doorway, the better for him to keep an eye on the road. He sat on the doorstep beside the food, tearing a tortilla, handing half to Capitán, who took it gently from him. "Que Dios se lo pague," he said to Ursula, who was just inside, slapping more corn dough between her hands. "May God repay you." He had said this to her three times a day for thirteen days. His only way of returning her generosity was to spend a few hours on the river and, if fate allowed, to bring back a few fish for her to blacken on the griddle.

He ate slowly. Periodically, he lifted his cup and blew across the coffee, and took a noisy cautious sip of the hot liquid. He could hear the voice of Servelia, his wife, reproaching him from the grave. "Niño, niño," she used to say, calling him "boy" when she thought he was acting like one. He had not been blessed with her for long. When Lety was eight, a year younger than the boy was now, she had lost her mother to el mal aire, the bad air that early morning can bring. In two days the fever had consumed her. Now the boy had lost his mother, too, and the thought of it was like a hand squeezing his heart. He shook his head and had to ask, Where are you, God, in all of this?

Ursula came to sit alongside him. She brought along her coffee cup. As he did each time she joined him, he said, "You don't have to sit here just because I do."

"I know," she said, looking down the street as well. "But I, too, want to see him when he comes around the corner."

The old man grunted, because it was all he could do to keep from crying. That she also was filled with hope meant much to him. He cleared his throat before saying, "I remember when Lety confessed she was having Nico. I guessed her condition the moment I saw her come over the hill. It was the way she came under the trees toward the rancho that told the story. She held her head high, my girl did. As if defying me. As if daring me to condemn what she had done." He took a slurp of coffee again. He set the cup down and continued. "She needn't have worried. Best thing she ever did was have that boy. For nine years, Nico's the reason I look forward to each morning."

Ursula nodded and took a sip from her own cup.

The two let their breakfasts and their thoughts settle. They kept their eyes steady on the road. Then the old man bunched up some frijoles with his fingers. He reached over to Capitán with them. "The dog's a beaner," he said.

"Aren't we all," Ursula replied.

twenty-eight

In the middle of the night, Nicolás knelt in the pantry with the door closed. He had taken his shirt off before sneaking in so he could block the crack along the bottom of the door. Then he had pulled on the light string. To work on the wall, he had to lie on his side with his legs drawn up. From this perspective, provisions sitting on the shelves seemed to teeter above him: bags of corn and beans and rice. Packets of manteca. Pans and bowls and pots stacked into towers. Chiles strung on a cord and hanging from a shelf edge. Pale papery garlic heads drooping down toward his own.

Outside and inside, all was quiet, and this spooked him. Enough so that he pulled the string again and plunged the pantry back into darkness. He didn't need the light. He could work on the wall by feel. Still, he would have welcomed the spot illumination of his flashlight. His tools were at hand: the Swiss army knife, the short crowbar, the big serving spoon borrowed from the kitchen. His fingers were familiar with the territory: the short reach to the wall, the crumbling plaster as he scraped and dug. The soft sound it made as it fell behind the shelf. Every now and then, his nose itched from the powdery plaster, forcing him to pause and wipe his face against a sweaty arm.

His plan was nearing realization. He had worked on the wall for three nights and had scraped the plaster from an area large enough for him to slip through. Tonight, he used the crowbar to pry away the lath, and now he could feel the plaster on the other side, and also found it soft and crumbly. Tomorrow night, he would use the crowbar again, and his legs as well, to break through to the other side and so find his way to freedom. Until that time, and as he had been since starting, he would be patient and cautious. He would take no chances. He would conceal his night work with stacks of little-used supplies. He would tiptoe over to the washbasin to rinse away any plaster dust before lying back down under the tree with the dogs. In the past three nights, how much had he slept? Ten, twelve hours?

He thought he heard footsteps. He stopped scraping and listened. Someone was in the kitchen. The refrigerator clicked open. After a moment, it closed. Very carefully, very quietly, he rose and stood against the wall, at the place where the door would conceal him if whoever was out there decided to open it. He waited. He could actually feel his heart thumping against the hand he placed over it. As if it were his machete, he grasped the crowbar in his other hand. He would use it if he had to. He prayed he didn't have to. Minutes passed. Was it Ofelia out there? No. She would have turned on the light. Whoever was there didn't wish to be seen. In a flash, he knew who it was. Vidal. Taking a side trip on his way back from the latrine. Footsteps again. The spigot at the sink going on. The water going off. More footsteps.

He willed himself not to move. After an eternity, he began to trust that the kitchen was empty. Only then did he drop down the pantry wall to sit there in the dark.

· · ·

The light awakened him. Beams of pearly light. He had seen this light before. In the cave. Was he there now? He shook his head to clear the sleep from it. "Tata?" he said. "Tata, are you there?"

"Nicolás, I am with you." That small soft voice.

He gasped. "Virgencita? Is it you?"

"I have come to help you."

He looked around. He was in the pantry, but it was close and hot like in the cave at home. Though he heard her voice, he could not see her. Only her mellow wavering light. "You helped me before," he said. "I had a dream. In my dream, you wrote ENTER HERE over the hidden door." He pointed beyond the glow, to where the top of the room was swallowed up by darkness. "See? Up there."

"Do not be afraid, Nicolás."

"I'm not afraid. I am brave."

"At noontime, Nicolás, you must be strong. You must be like the lion."

"At noon?"

"At noontime, be alert."

"When?"

"I am with you, Nicolás."

"I know."

"At noontime you will see me. Follow me to safety."

The radiance flickered like the flame at the end of a candle stub. "Don't go," he said, but there was no answer. Only the darkness again. Only his questions.

twenty-nine

Nicolás rose with the soldiers at reveille. He stood very straight at roll call and saluted the flag as it climbed up the pole. Despite little sleep, he did his jumping-jacks and push-ups with vigor, pumping himself up with every repetition. To what end, he did not know. Whatever noontime brought his way, he would be ready for it. He ate his breakfast hastily, something not lost on Ofelia. "What are you rushing for?" she inquired. "You look like you're being chased." He left the kitchen as if he were, and tugged the hose out to the sidewalk where he could keep a better eye on things. Our Lady's warning had given him eyes at the back of his head. Had provided extra ears with which to hear.

At mid-morning, another group of soldiers readied themselves for target practice. Nicolás was sweeping the corridor when the sergeant came around the corner. Nicolás rested the broom against his shoulder. He asked if he were to carry the ammunition as he had before.

"It's your lucky day," the sergeant said. "Someone else will be the pack mule today."

Nicolás nodded. It was only right. Today he was a lion.

He watched them march out of the garrison, past the oil drum barricade, down the middle of the street. Sergeant, lieutenant, and twelve soldiers. A guard stood post on the corner, and he, too, watched his comrades march away. "You want to be a soldier like them?" he asked Nicolás.

Nicolás threw up his shoulders. He did not want to be a soldier. He wanted to save lives.

"You keep up the good work and, before you know it, you'll be in uniform. In a good pair of boots."

I already have boots, Nicolás thought.

"And you'll have yourself a rifle." The soldier's weapon was slung at his side. He patted it tenderly. "That was quite a day when I got mine."

La niña Rocío poked her head out of her store. "Chelito," she said, "you're just what I need. Come in here and help me."

"I'll be in there," Nicolás said to the soldier.

The store was filled with a fragrance he had not noticed in the place before. "It smells good in here," he said.

"It's the roses." She pointed to the glass jar sprouting blood-red blossoms on the counter. "Come take a sniff." She was sitting on her stool behind the counter. She waved him over.

"That's okay," he said, because it was not manly to stick your nose into flowers.

"Suit yourself. Anyway, look what I did. I dropped my key and it slid under there." She pointed, but he had to go around the counter to see exactly where.

"Where?"

"Under the shelf. I'd get it myself, but—¡Uy! I don't like sticking my arm into a place where I can't see. You never know what your hand is going to fall upon."

Nicolás squatted next to the shelf. The area she indicated was just above the place he would break into tonight. It was a miracle. Now he had an opportunity to take a close look at this side of his escape route. Was this Our Lady's doing? He reached under the shelf, smoothing his blind hand across the floor, and found the key at once. He held it for a moment before bringing it out. He used the time to inspect the items on the shelf: stacked boxes containing packets of aspirin and digestive powders. It was going to be easy. He would simply push aside the boxes when he broke through. "Here's your key," he said, standing up and placing it on the counter. He brushed the dust and grime from his arm.

She gave a little shudder. "¡Uy! I don't see how you can do that."

"Do what?"

"Stick your arm under there."

He was starting out the door when she said, "Wait a minute. Before you go, pick out a piece of candy for your trouble. Pick whatever kind you want."

He turned back and looked through the top of the counter, tapping a finger over the jar of caramels inside. "I like caramels."

Without leaving the stool, she lowered her head and reached an arm into the back of the case. Her head was so near, he could see the part of her hair. It was like a road running down the middle of her scalp. She bobbed back up. "Here. Have two. You did a brave thing."

He reached past the roses for the candy wrapped in blue paper twists. "Gracias, niña Rocío." He put them in his pocket, next to his little wooden lion.

He was halfway down the sidewalk when he remembered a story his mother often told. A long, long time ago, in Mexico, la Virgen de Guadalupe appeared to an Indian, Juan Diego. On the hill where her figure stood, blood-red roses bloomed. He looked back over his shoulder at the store. The flowers. The key. The shelf. His eyes so near the path to freedom. It was la Virgen's doing. And it wasn't even noon.

•   •   •

At ten after twelve, the thirty soldiers not at target practice were in the dining hall enjoying roasted beef smothered in a sauce rich with tomatoes. Thirty rifles rested in the racks lining the corridor wall. Ofelia bustled in and out of the kitchen, as did Silvia, both of them serving platters of sautéed vegetables and rice with petit pois. Hoping for a handout, Principe and Princesa visited each soldier's place; they kept out of Ofelia's path, lest she wallop them with a foot.

At the washbasin, Chabela was having a smoke, her hands momentarily dry and at rest.

As was the custom, el capitán Portillo had had his lunch before the soldiers ate. He now sat at his desk, his back to the window and to the oil drums blocking the street. He was finishing a report and looking forward to his twenty-minute siesta. His right-hand man, Lieutenant Galindo, was away. He had backed the jeep out past the wide back doors of the garrison and driven it over to the approved service center to have the differential checked.

Vidal had been on duty at the entrance and his tour was coming to an end. Good thing, he thought, for his appetite was piqued by the odors wafting from the kitchen. In her store, la niña Rocío perched on her stool. Swathed in the scent of roses, she swayed in rhythm to the love song floating from the radio.

Nicolás washed his hands at the bathroom sink. Moments before, he had been in the kitchen, his plate before him at the table, but he had bolted because his stomach cramped up. He did not know the cause. Maybe it was the smell of the beef, but that had never unsettled him before. Maybe it was the lack of sleep.

Across town, a panel truck, at a prudent speed, rolled down the Calle Central toward the garrison. In its rear, ten guerrilleros crowded, all heavily armed, all with bandannas masking the bottom halves of their faces.

Thirty more like them approached on foot from the north and the south, some with rifles tucked at their sides or under their shirts, all with bandannas stuffed under their shirt collars.

Three men strolled down the sidewalk in front of the garrison. They walked casually, naturally, until two were at the corners and the third at the entrance. With his left hand, the man at the entrance tipped his hat to Vidal and said, "Buenas tardes, señor oficial." With his right hand he pulled a pistol from his trousers and shot Vidal in the chest at point-blank range. The two men at the corners killed the soldiers there in like fashion. Immediately after their shots sounded, three guerilleros sprayed the guards at the rear of the building with bursts from AK-47s.

The sound of gunfire sent the soldiers at the table jumping to their feet and scurrying for their rifles. As they did, the panel truck screamed around a corner and sped through the back entrance, braking right in front of Chabela's washstand. The doors flew open and the men leaped out, weapons at the ready but not yet firing, because the whole scenario had unfolded in just forty-five seconds and the soldiers had not yet made it to the patio. Meanwhile, more guerrilleros on foot charged in through both the front and back entrances.

The first to offer resistance was Captain Portillo. He leaned out the doorway of his office and expertly shot down two guerrilleros before he was riddled by an AK-47. Then some of the soldiers appeared and the exchange of gunfire became stupendously loud. Hit bodies flew and spun and lurched. Among them Chabela, a cigarette still between her fingers, who took a bullet in the back just as she reached the kitchen door.

In the kitchen, Ofelia screamed and implored to God in heaven. In the dining room, Silvia slipped on the tomato sauce that had spilled on the floor from the platter she was holding. She tried to scamper up but slipped again. She finally rolled under the table with the dogs, an act that ultimately saved her.

Nicolás had come out of the bathroom. He was in an inner hall, and for a moment the noise around him was so loud, it paralyzed him. A second explosion shocked the building. He threw his hands over his head as parts of the ceiling rained down on him. He ran for the kitchen and pushed through the back door. He stopped in his tracks at what he beheld: half the ceiling was on the floor, and half of a wall. The stove, the refrigerator, the table with his lunch, all lay under beams and tiles and hunks of plaster. Little fires blazed in spots. Ofelia poked up from one of the mounds of debris. Blood streamed down her face. She shrieked and waved her arms as if caught in the roil of an ocean wave. Nicolás picked his way over the rubble to help her. Above the uproar, he made out what she was clamoring: "It was you! You informed on us! All day you acted strange!"

Nicolás wheeled away from her. Toward the pantry, its door flung open. He could see the shelves, crowded with provisions. He heard the cracks of rifles and pistols and the explosions from grenades. Orders were shouted. The sound of heavy scrambling and footsteps was everywhere. Above it all, Nicolás heard Our Lady's voice: "You are a lion. Eres un león." In the pantry, his escape route beckoned.

Nicolás took a deep breath and gathered the din into himself. Another breath. He bared his teeth. He lifted his arms that were like paws, his fingers that were like claws. He growled. A deep rumbling rose from his chest and filled him with ferocity; it propelled him through the pantry door. He yanked on the light string, but no light came on. No matter. He could do this blindfolded. He pulled supplies from the lower shelves and flung them out into the kitchen. Pots and pans clattered onto the wreckage already in the room. Corn and beans and rice showered from hurled bags. He worked feverishly, dropping down on his rump when the area he needed was cleared. He thrust his legs over the shelf and kicked away at the wall. One hard drive. Another. A third. The plaster gave way. One of his boots pushed through. He kept on kicking until light from the store spilled into the pantry, until the square of light looked wide enough to swallow him.

He flipped over on his belly then, ignoring Ofelia's weakening screams and the chaos coming from beyond the kitchen. He scooted over the shelf, the plaster dust thick in his throat and blinding his eyes. He wiped them clear, then reached through the wall into the store and shoved aside the supplies on the lower shelf. He grasped the edge of it and pulled himself forward. He used a fishtail motion and wiggled through, little by little. Halfway in, he saw that the storekeeper was gone. Her stool lay on its side behind the counter. Her radio was playing. The door to the street stood open.

He was almost through. A barrage of shots tore into the kitchen behind him. The store counter was just an arm's length away; Nicolás took hold of its leg and used it as a counterweight to pull himself all the way in. He cleared the width of the shelf. He rose and scrambled for the door. Bullets smashed through the wall of the pantry. Shelving collapsed. The glass counter shattered.

He was at the door when something shoved him so forcefully forward that he went down on all fours. At first he thought he had tripped on the door frame, but then his side was burning and he reached and touched it and his hand came away with blood. He got up again and stumbled outside. Vidal was sprawled on the sidewalk. A guerrillero lay at the entrance, lines of his blood spilling onto the pavement. The street's businesses had slammed shut their doors. Shoppers cowered in doorways. Up the street, the metal doors of the poster shop were still open. On one of the doors hung the image of la Virgen Milagrosa.

Nicolás locked his eyes on the sweet milky face of his benefactress. He staggered across the street. He thought he saw beams of light coming from her little hands. A long sidewalk loomed before him. Another street after that. Then the street of the lilac house. He held his side and ran painfully toward it. Not once did he look back.

thirty

When the street door of the lilac house cracked open, Nicolás gasped, "Help me," and pushed his way in when the woman there hesitated. "El señor Alvarado, please." Nicolás choked out the words because he was breathless and his side was on fire. "I've been shot." He lifted a bloody palm toward her in proof. She took a step back.

"What is it?" Alvarado himself said. Across an entry patio, he stood framed in the doorway of the house, a napkin tucked into the opening of his shirt like a gigantic white tie. A pistol butt poked out of his waistband.

"Señor, remember me? I'm Nicolás Veras. I was here a few weeks ago. You helped me write a letter to my mother. Look. I've been shot." He turned his hand over again, feeling the strength drain away from him. He went down on a knee. In the distance came another explosion followed by bursts of automatic weapons.

Alvarado rushed over. "Clara, bolt the door. From now on, don't open it to anyone." He pulled Nicolás upright and lifted him carefully into his arms. He carried him over the patio and into the house, through the living room with the round table and chairs and the refrigerator in the corner. He set him down on a daybed under the windows looking out on a patio. "Let's get the shirt off," Alvarado said.

Gingerly, Nicolás pulled his shirt from the waistband of his jeans. The side and tail of the shirt were blood-soaked. His blood was startlingly red. "I'll get it on everything."

"Don't worry about that." Alvarado took the shirt and handed it to Clara, who had followed them into the room. "Lay down," he said. He plucked the napkin from his chest and pressed the cloth to Nicolás's side.

Nicolás winced. "Am I going to die?"

"I can't tell yet." Alvarado daubed away the blood. His woolly eyebrows shifted as he furrowed his brow and examined the wound.

Nicolás waited a moment before asking, "Can you tell now?"

At length, Alvarado said, "Good news. You're going to live. You were lucky. The bullet only grazed you. Looks like it whizzed right under your arm. It's a miracle, really."

It was la Virgen, Nicolás thought.

"I'll get a pan of water and the medical supplies," Clara said.

With his free hand, Alvarado pulled the pistol from his waistband and placed it on a table. He drew a chair close and dropped down on it. With the other hand, he kept pressure on the wound. "This'll soon stop bleeding. When it does, I'll clean and disinfect it. Then I'll wrap it up."

Nicolás nodded, his mind awash with images of the rancho and the string cots holding Chema and his putrid stomach wound. He saw himself fanning flies from Chema's wound. He pictured Samuel lying on another cot, his shattered leg resting against the incline of the ramp Dr. Eddy had rigged up. Chema and Samuel. Elías and Gerardo. El gringo and Dr. Felix. It seemed so long ago since he had known these men.

Clara hurried in. She was short and dark. How old, he could not tell. Nicolás watched her ready the supplies. He could tell she had done this before. She dunked a clean cloth into the pan of water, wrung it out, and handed it to Alvarado.

"So tell me, Nicolás. How did you come to be wounded?" As he spoke, Alvarado did not look up from his work.

"Did you hear the commotion? Out there in the street? It was the garrison. The guerrillas attacked it."

"So they did."

Nicolás looked more closely at Alvarado. The man's face was a stone. Only his eyebrows provided any movement. The way he uttered the words "So they did," it was as if he had known of the attack. If this were true, would someone soon come banging on Alvarado's door? But no. Nicolás could not worry about such things. He must remember el señor's kindness: the tangerines, the writing tablet, his company all the way to the post office. Nicolás had to rely on such kindness today. He had nothing else to do. Whatever he was asked, he would tell the truth.

"And how did you come to be wounded?" Alvarado asked again.

"It started two weeks ago, at the rancho. The guerrillas heard the army was out on a sweep. They went off into the hills. My grandfather and I hid in the cave. When the army came, they burned the rancho and captured me. They brought me to the garrison. I was held there until now. During the attack, I managed to run out of the building and escape, but as you see, I was shot."

"Who did it? Do you know?"

Nicolás shrugged. "It was either the army or the guerrillas. In the end, they're all the same."

"And your grandfather? What happened to him?"

"The army didn't get him. He was in the cave while I was at the river. That was two weeks ago, so I don't know where he is. But once we made a vow, my grandfather and me. If we were separated, we would meet at the church in El Retorno."

"What about your mother? I mailed your letter. Did she ever answer it?"

"My mother is dead." It was the first time he had uttered this, and he was surprised that the words sounded so matter-of-fact.

"Monseñor's funeral mass, if I recall correctly."

It touched Nicolás that Alvarado had remembered this. To make his mother real, he went on to speak of her. "Her name was Lety Veras. She worked for la niña Flor de Salah. In San Salvador."

Alvarado nodded. He uncorked a bottle filled with amber liquid. He dunked a cotton swab into it. "This is going to burn." Clara picked up a section of newspaper lying on the table and stirred the air with it. Nicolás bit his lip. He did not cry out when the swab touched his flesh. Nor when Alvarado squeezed a sharp-smelling unguent directly on the wound, nor when he pressed a thick bandage to it. He stood, teetering a bit as Alvarado wrapped his torso round and round with gauze. His brow broke out in sweat, and he swiped it with a hand. "It hurts." He slowly lowered himself onto the side of the bed.

"I'll give you something for that," Alvarado said.

"But I can't stay. The cook at the garrison thinks I'm an

informer." He remembered that now: Ofelia's upper half poking out of the rubble in the kitchen. Ofelia shrieking out the news. The little fires burning around her.

"You're safe with us." Alvarado shook a pill out of a vial. "Here, take this." Clara provided a glass a water. After he swallowed the pill, she took hold of the palm he had laid against his side and wiped it free of blood with another moist cloth. She wiped his face, too, chalky with plaster dust. "You rest," she said, and she pulled his boots off and pressed him down till he was prone. "While you sleep, I'll see if I can find you another shirt."

Nicolás closed his eyes, too exhausted to resist. He imagined himself on his river, floating on the current, looking up at the sky. Carry me, river, he thought; and he let the river take him to a place where there were no guns, no soldiers, no guerrilleros. Only Our Lady up there in the clouds, shining down on him.

· · ·

Evening came. On the daybed under the windows, the boy still slept. Alvarado sat smoking in the gloom. So as not to disturb the boy, he had lit only one lamp. It cast a mellow light over him in the easy chair, on the desk and the radio, turned on low. He sat listening to the reports about the noontime guerrilla attack. The official story was that the army had killed a great number of guerrilleros. That they had repulsed their attackers and kept them from confiscating weapons from the armory. That one soldier had been killed, and two servants, a cook and a laundress. In reality, twenty soldiers were killed and six guerrilleros. The cook and the laundress, three civilians in the wrong place at the wrong time, were added casualties. The armory was broken into. A panel truck loaded with arms and ammunition made a clean getaway.

The phone rang, a shrill report, and Alvarado laid his cigarette in the ashtray and snatched the receiver off its cradle. "¿Bueno?"

"Señor Alvarado? Basilio Fermín in San Salvador. You called earlier and talked to a fellow servant. She said you have Nicolás Veras."

"Yes, the boy is here."

"The boy's mother worked for my employer. We've been looking for him for weeks, since his mother was killed. The boy's grandfather was here not long ago. He said the boy had disappeared. He thought the boy might have come here, but he hadn't."

"Is the grandfather still there?"

"No. He left and went back home. He said he would wait for the boy in El Retorno. At the church."

"The boy mentioned that."

"How is Nicolás?"

"He was being kept by the army here in Tejutla. The garrison was attacked today. He was wounded."

"How bad?"

"Not seriously. Only a flesh wound. He's sleeping now."

"I'll come for him in the morning. My patrona, la niña Flor de Salah, will provide for him. For the grandfather, too. If the roads aren't blocked, I'll try to get up to El Retorno."

"I should expect you in the morning, then?"

"I'll be there."

The telephone had awakened Nicolás. Because he was groggy, he had trouble following what was said. Still, it was clear he was being talked about. In the morning, someone was coming to take him away. Who? he could not guess. No matter. He would not allow himself to be captured again. He would not be caught in the middle of anything again. He knew what he must do. Stay very still. Pretend to sleep. When Alvarado and the woman retired, he would slip out and disappear.

• • •

Through the window of the darkened room, the half-moon laid a yellow rectangle upon the daybed, upon the table with the medical supplies, the pills, the tall glass of water. On the chair Alvarado had drawn up to the bed, a T-shirt lay folded. Nicolás propped himself on an elbow. He looked down at the white gauze circling his chest. He probed the bandage with a finger. The wound felt tight. When he moved, the skin stretched and there was pain in that. He swung his legs onto the floor and rested for a moment, listening. The refrigerator hummed in the corner. He stood and grabbed the T-shirt. It seemed blue in the moonlight and looked quite big. He pulled it on, leaving it loose over his waist. He snatched the vial of pills and slipped it into his pocket, his fingers touching the caramels that had been his prize for being brave. He unwrapped one and ate it in two bites. The sweet candy clung to his teeth. He gulped down the water in the glass. He struggled with his boots, difficult to pull on without bending over. In the end, he unloosened the laces and slipped his feet in, tucking the laces in around the tongues as best he could. He searched for the pistol that Alvarado had laid on the table, but the pistol was not there. Because he had seen wounds turn bad, Nicolás picked up a handful of gauze bandages and the tube of smelly unguent.

He would leave the house through the back. From the trip he had made with Gerardo and Elías, he remembered the woods not far from the house. He tiptoed across the living room. Past the round table that once held a bowl of fragrant tangerines. He stepped into a short hall. Deep snores came from somewhere down the end of it. He went in the opposite direction and slowly pushed open a door he prayed was the kitchen. He poked his head in. Weak light came from a tiny bulb set in the wall over a counter. He made out the contours of the stove. A table. A window. The back door. He stepped into the room, hoping to find something he could take with him to eat. He had had nothing since breakfast. And that he had gulped down.

He was feeling along the counter when a figure materialized in the corner, next to the door. "Where are you going?" the figure said.

Nicolás took in a breath that was so loud he was startled even more. To steady himself, he held on to the counter.

The figure stepped fully into the room. "It is I. Don't be afraid."

She was enveloped in shadows, so he could not make out her features, only the light-colored tunic she wore that dropped down to the floor.

"Where are you going?" she repeated.

"I have to find my grandfather."

In the dimness, he thought he saw her nod.

"Are you hungry? You had no dinner."

"Sí," he answered.

"Wait here." She whisked past him and out the door into the hall.

For a moment, Nicolás hesitated, perplexed by the apparition. He was about to bolt toward the door when she returned. "Here's some cheese. A few apples. Some tortillas. They were in the refrigerator." She opened up a cabinet and took something down. "And here are some cookies. You like cookies, don't you? These are my favorites."

He could only nod.

She reached under the counter and pulled out something in which she placed the food. From the rustling sounds, he realized it was a plastic bag. He watched her tie up the end. She handed it to him. "Vaya."

"Grácias."

"Go," she said. "Take your time. Rest along the way."

"Sí."

"You're a brave boy, Nicolás." She opened the back door to the night and to the moonlight. She did not step into the light. He moved past her, catching the scent of something vaguely familiar, something he could not readily place.

He was halfway to the woods when it struck him what it was. Roses. She smelled of roses, the symbol of la Virgen. Nicolás looked back toward the house. It had happened again: to give him heart, Our Lady had appeared to him.

thirty-one

Just after daybreak, the old man waded into the tepid waters of the Sumpul. He threw in a line, hoping for plenty of fish. Resting on the bank, his turquoise pail waited for the catch. Capitán was fishing, too. He snapped at minnows darting just under the water. The old man called the fish in, something he always did, but in his head, where it was safe to have such conversations. And they *were* conversations, for the fish frequently responded when he spoke to them. Today he said, "Oh, fish, come to me. You are needed for Ursula's griddle." When no fish answered, he added enticements. "The people of El Retorno are hungry. There's Paulina from the little store. Emilio Sánchez. Pablo and even Delfina from the pharmacy. Come, fish, calm the people's hunger. Come to me and fulfill your destiny."

At length, the fish spoke back. They said, "It is a grand thing, destiny. Certainly we will consider your request," but they did not rush to his beckoning hook. Still, despite the fishes' restraint, the old man knew it was only patience that stood between him and a filled turquoise pail.

The sun climbed past the tops of the trees lining the op-

posite bank. Honduran trees there. Over them, the sky was
a serpentine of rose and lavender, a soft bluing in between.
The old man recalled a terrifying morning, eleven years back.
He had been in Honduras, where he had spent several
months working as a laborer at a cattle ranch. It had been
July, well into winter. Heavy rains eroded the land. Land-
slides closed roads. The river was at flood stage, and the
place where he now stood would have been entirely under
water. Because of the storms, the fences at the cattle ranch
were in constant need of repair. To mend them, he had sunk
an endless supply of new posts and retacked lengths of
barbed wire between them. He had the scars to prove it:
puncture marks along his arms that had faded to gray freck-
les; the long jagged gash across his right thigh.

Back then, following a viciously fought soccer match,
war had erupted between El Salvador and Honduras. Salvadorans working across the border had been driven back
across the river by armed Guardia bent on insuring that the
scarce jobs available to their citizens were not taken by for-
eigners. It was the story of his life: caught always in between.

At a place near La Arada, a day's walk downstream, he
had crossed the Sumpul. To save himself, he had risked the
river's fury: the current roiling and fierce, the swollen river
awash with dislodged boulders and with the shattered sections of trees unfortunate enough to grow near the bank.
With the Guardia at his back, he had stepped into the roar-
ing river. It had swept him away. He had been holding his
machete aloft. It was strapped to his wrist and sheathed in
its scabbard, but the current snapped the thong in an instant
like he'd heard the big fish can snap lines at sea.

He rode the mad river for almost a kilometer, bobbing
and whooshing and bumping over rocks and around debris.

Muddy water clogging his mouth, his eyes, his nose. The deafening noise drowning out all other sounds. It was a tangle of brush that netted him like a fish and miraculously slowed him down. He had spent frantic moments fighting the current that sought to pull him under. He held on tight. Reaching hand over hand, he used the clot of vegetation to lead him to safety. When he made it to the bank his sandals were gone; the right leg of his trousers was completely torn away. But that was long ago, when he was a vigorous man of fifty-five. A man in his full powers.

So engrossed had he been in the past that he was not aware of Capitán barking wildly behind him. The old man heard the dog now, and turned toward the riverbank.

Standing there, as if by magic, was his grandson.

"Tata," Nicolás said.

thirty-two

Nicolás and Tata collided into each other's arms. They did not speak; instead they sobbed. Tata silently, Nicolás in noisy bursts that tightened his throat and stung his eyes. Capitán whined and circled them, his back end swaying like a dancer's.

"Vaya, hijo, vaya," Tata said at length. He wiped his eyes with the back of a hand. "Here. Let me look at you."

Nicolás lifted the hem of his shirt and dried his tears. "They shot me, Tata." He raised the shirt higher for his grandfather to see.

"Who? Where?"

"At the garrison. It was either the soldiers or the guerrillas."

Tata bent over and examined the wide gauze around Nicolás's torso. "Dios Santo, we need to find a doctor."

Nicolás shook his head. "El señor Alvarado from the health center at Tejutla fixed me up. He said it wasn't serious. He said it was a flesh wound." Nicolás lowered his shirt and pointed to the plastic bag lying on the riverbank. "There's medicine in there."

"Let's get over to Ursula's," Tata said. "She'll have some

breakfast and you can rest. Delfina from the pharmacy can take a look at you."

"I walked all night. I was going to the church. I stopped at the river for a drink, and there you were, Tata." The sight of his grandfather had banished his exhaustion.

Tata smiled for the first time in almost three weeks. He clasped Nicolás's shoulder and gently pulled him close. "I've been waiting for you, boy."

•   •   •

All of El Retorno's population came out to welcome Nicolás: Ursula, Delfina, who had owned the pharmacy; and Paulina, who had owned the store. Emilio, who was rebuilding his mechanic's shop; and Don Pablo, whose house had been destroyed and who was now living with Emilio. All five people put their hands together and turned their eyes to heaven, exclaiming what a miracle it was that he had returned. They overwhelmed him with questions, insisting on seeing his wound when he told of his shooting. Delfina, the closest thing they had to a doctor, squeezed fresh unguent on it and redressed it. Nicolás was relieved to see that the wound did not look red or puffy, a sign of infection. One of the many things he had learned from Felix and the big gringo, Eddy. Don Pablo leaned over and felt Nicolás's arm muscle. "You've filled out, boy."

"They make you work hard in the army," Nicolás said.

"Looks like they fed you good, too," Ursula said. "There's more flesh on your bones than I've seen before."

"They feed you," Nicolás said, not caring to go into detail. A wave of fatigue washed suddenly over him.

"Well, this isn't the army," Ursula said, "but I have tortillas and beans and plenty of coffee."

"I just need a drink of water," Nicolás said. He had been thirsty since daybreak.

Ursula fetched a glass, and Nicolás drank the water down in one long gulp. He drank a second glass, then a third.

"You'll be peeing all day," Paulina said. She was standing near the door, her arms crossed over her belly.

Tata sat down on the doorstep beside his grandson. "Don't you want something to eat?"

"I want to sleep."

Ursula said, "You can have the place in back where you used to stay."

"Where are you staying, Tata?"

"In the church. I brought la Virgen from the cave. She's back in her niche."

"That's where I want to be."

• • •

Nicolás slept all day. He stirred at dusk, as the votive candles Ursula had placed in Our Lady's niche were starting to cast some light on the surroundings. The section of tree that had fallen against the altar had been hauled out, and now the altar was but a broken-down wall of empty, dusty recesses. Emilio Sánchez, when he had used the church for an abode, had pulled the broken pews into the yard and cleared the place of rubble. Because the church was now devoid of furniture and its western wall, the approaching night tiptoed into the church with nothing to stop it.

"You're awake," Tata said. He sat against the wall where for some time he had been keeping the boy company. Nicolás raised his head when Tata spoke. He rubbed his forehead and yawned. "I fell asleep."

"You needed your rest."

Nicolás propped himself up on an elbow. He lifted his chin in the direction of the bundle that was near the altar. "Is that my backpack, Tata?"

"I carried the statue in it. I brought your machete and flashlight, too. Also that little wooden lamb Basilio Fermín carved. The lion, I couldn't find."

Nicolás raised his hip and patted his jeans pocket. "I have it here. I took it with me when I left the cave to get water. It was to help me be strong."

"Well, you've been strong all right."

"Did you get your fish, Tata?" The turquoise pail was sitting beside the backpack.

"I caught some fish while you were sleeping. Ursula fried them up. We can go down and have them."

Nicolás sat up with his back against the wall. He felt stiff and his side hurt. He looked across the church, at the enormous shadow of the conacaste. "The tree looks sad."

"These hard times make everything look sad." Tata was silent for a moment, then added, "How's your side?"

Nicolás shrugged. "It's sore, but the ointment is helping me."

"In the morning, if you think you can do it, we will go down to Dulce Nombre de María and get on the bus to San Salvador."

"Why?"

"Because a doctor needs to look at you."

"Are we going to la niña Flor's?"

Tata nodded. "After you disappeared, I went to her house. I talked to Basilio Fermín, and he said the Salah family wants to take care of you."

Nicolás shook his head slowly. Events were taking shape

that he could not control, and he felt like a river stone tossed about in swift current. He turned his gaze away from his grandfather. There was something he needed to say, and he steeled himself and took a deep breath before saying it.

"Mamá is dead, Tata." Nicolás uttered the words quietly to soften their blow. He threw his arms around himself, because the knowledge of this had been a weight. Now that he had told the truth to another, he thought he might float up off the dusty floor of the church and vanish over its tumble-down remains.

"I know. I found her shoe in your backpack. Also, Basilio told me."

"What did he say?"

"He took me to her grave. They buried her in a place with white tombstones and white angels sitting on top of them."

"Does Mamá's grave have an angel?"

"No. It has a little statue of la Virgen Milagrosa."

Nicolás nodded.

"Your mother loved Our Lady."

They sat saying nothing for a time. They watched the shadows deepen. The night bestowed a sweetness to the air, and they tried to take it in, the better to shake off the mood that had befallen them.

"I saw la Virgen last night," Nicolás said at length. "She wore a long white gown. She gave me cookies. They're in the plastic bag. She said they were her favorites."

"You're a fortunate boy that Our Lady shows herself to you."

"Es cierto. It's true."

Tata stood and shook his legs out. "How about a little fish?" he said. They walked wearily toward Ursula's. They descended the hill from the church, looking carefully so as not to stumble in the ruts and holes left by the air attack.

• • •

Capitán and Emilio's dog gingerly picked over the fish heads Ursula had thrown into the street for them. The townfolk congregated in her doorway for a chat after dinner, since Ursula's was the only place in town illuminated by electricity. A lightbulb hanging from a cord set in the room's ceiling spilled the precious light past the entrance and into the street. It wasn't that electricity did not flow to El Retorno, it was just that in the previous army sweep, bulbs, sockets, and plugs had been destroyed. The lamp posts set at each end of town were still standing, but their lamps had been shattered and no replacements were to be found, nor was there money to buy them. Had there been ready money, it would not have mattered: they lacked the ladder needed to install them. When Ursula hiked up the hill toward home, she carried her 40-watt lightbulb as if it were cupped water.

Still the center of attention, Nicolás was discomfited by it. He did not wish to be rude, for these were his elders and, as such, he was obliged to them, but the truth was, he did not wish to talk about the things they wished to know: the guerrillas, the army, weapons, tactics. En fin, everything. To dissuade them, he kept his answers short. When Capitán lifted his head from the fish bones and started to growl, Nicolás was at first pleased by it, but then the nature of the interruption sounded an alert. "What is it, Capitán?" The dog was standing stiff-legged and was looking down the street, past the circle of light Ursula's single bulb cast outdoors.

"What is it, boy?" Tata said. He stared down the street.

All the people did. From somewhere beyond the light an unfamiliar voice called out, "Please hold your animals."

Machete in hand, Emilio Sánchez stepped away from the others. "Who goes there?"

"It's only us." It was a woman's voice.

The dogs pricked up their ears and began to bark.

"Hold them back! There are children here."

"Who are you?" Emilio said. The dogs were at his side as if waiting for a signal. Threats rumbled in their throats.

"We're from San Francisco Morazán. Security forces burned us out. We've been on the move all day."

Emilio shushed the dogs and restrained his own. Tata stepped up and held Capitán back.

"Show yourselves," Emilio said.

A little girl, perhaps three or four, walked into the light. A woman followed. Then a small boy.

The woman held her hands up as if to allay any fears. "It's only us. Please hold the dogs back."

"They'll settle down." Emilio and Tata held tight to the animals. They petted away their barks and growls.

The woman pointed to the darkness behind her. "There's more of us coming. We're the first. This girl of mine can run."

"I'm hungry," the girl said. She had skinny pigtails. Her nose was snotty. Grime covered her arms and legs.

Before long, five others made their presence known: two more women and three men. One of them was Basilio Fermín.

thirty-three

The new arrivals brought disturbing news: because the guerrillas had attacked the army garrison in Tejutla, security forces were combing the area for those responsible. On foot and by air, the army was sweeping the region clean of insurgents capable of further assaults. People from El Común had fled their homes, as had those from San Francisco Morazán, from San Rafael as well. All were fleeing north to escape the operatives coming from the south.

The people gathered in Ursula's doorway, attracted by her single lightbulb and because she was handing out tortillas. Basilio Fermín was the newcomers' spokesman. That he was dressed in city clothes, wore lace-up shoes, and had a Panama hat had earned him that authority. That he had a gun provided another reason.

"Lucky we ran into him," said one of the newcomers, a man who appeared to be in his thirties. "Don Basilio has a pistol. We're lucky he's one of us."

Basilio said he had learned of the sweep this morning from el señor Alvarado. He had gone to Alvarado's in search of Nicolás and, finding that he had left, correctly surmised that he had returned to El Retorno. Basilio drove as far as Dulce Nombre de María, where he had been obliged to abandon his car. "There were many roadblocks," he said. "Guardia and police everywhere. How I managed to evade them is a miracle. I did not want to push my luck, so I parked the car on a side street and set off on foot."

Nicolás had mixed emotions about Basilio's presence here. He was fond of the man; after all, he had worked with his mother, had been one of her friends. But it was also true that Basilio's intent was to take him back to San Salvador, and while he was eager to leave the chaos of the countryside, he had no desire to be separated from his grandfather.

"What are we going to do now?" Tata asked, as if reading Nicolás's mind. "This boy here was wounded yesterday. I need to get him to San Salvador."

"I'm okay, Tata," Nicolás said lamely, for his grandfather's declaration was embarrassing.

"What do you mean he was wounded?" said Basilio.

"I'm okay," Nicolás repeated. He lifted the edge of his shirt. "I'm all bandaged and everything. El señor Alvarado said it was a flesh wound." He lowered his shirt as if to end discussion of the matter.

Basilio said, "Your grandfather's right. You must see a doctor. But we can't get to San Salvador over the regular routes. Not at the present, we can't."

"How about El Carrizal?" someone else offered. "There's a people's clinic there."

Nicolás thought, That's where el gringo Eddy is.

Paulina from the little store chimed in, "Hard as it is, we all should leave. The army bombed us out six weeks ago because of the guerrillas. Then they burned your place, Don Tino," she said to Tata. "It's only a matter of days before the soldiers are back."

"Paulina's right," Ursula said. "We should follow the river to La Arada. That's just a day's walk. We can cross the river there. There's a refugee camp in Honduras not far from there."

"I've crossed at that spot before," Tata said. "Or tried to cross, I should say. The river was flooding and it took me for a ride."

"No chance of that now," Paulina said. "The rainy season is still weeks away."

Don Pablo said, "I'm not leaving again. I'm staying put, no matter what."

"Me too," Emilio Sánchez said. "I didn't leave before, and I'm sure as hell not leaving now." He pointed to the dogs. "I'll stay here with the mutts. Taking a dog would not be prudent. A dog's bark could give a person away."

Tata nodded his agreement. "What about you?" he asked Basilio.

"Where you and the boy go, I go too," Basilio replied.

All had their say as they voiced the pros and cons of fleeing, proposing various routes they would take if they did. In the end, all but Don Pablo and Emilio decided to go. They would follow the river toward Ojo de Agua, near the hamlet of La Arada where the river could be crossed nearest to the Honduran camp. On the way, they would stop at El Carrizal, where the clinic would see to Nicolás's wound. If they left now, they could travel under the cover of night. If all went as planned, they would reach their destination by nightfall tomorrow.

thirty-four

From the left came the revolutionaries, the guerrillas. Seeking allegiance, recruits, provisions, and safe harbor amid the anonymity of the general populace, they were swift to take action against those who denied their needs or betrayed their cause.

From the right came the army, the Guardia, and the paramilitary forces of Orden, pursuing the guerrillas and eradicating sympathizers, real or imagined.

Caught in the perilous between were the people. Dying in the crossfire of weapons and ideologies. Agonizing over loved ones slain or tortured. Weeping over destroyed homes and ravaged possessions. Cornered in a flood of menace and fear, there was nothing left for them to do but flee.

At the sound of distant fire, at the faraway rumble of airplanes or the sonorous thump of helicopters, the people gathered their belongings and abandoned their ranchos and shacks and one-room houses. They joined their neighbors and took to the hills. They traveled at night, if there was time enough to wait for it. They followed well-worn paths that meandered through the ragged, uneven terrain, tethering themselves in long lines with lengths of cord or with their belts in order to stay together. By day, they kept under the trees or close to whatever vegetation might provide them with cover. They watched each other's backs, praying they would not stumble into an ambush by either the right or the left.

The people quit their homes in small groups that joined with others to form larger groups. These grew to a multitude marching on with one common aim: to evade whatever peril fate placed before them, to reach La Arada and cross the Sumpul River to safety.

The people came from towns and villages and hamlets. They came from San Francisco Morazán and Los Encuentros. From Los Amates and Cuevitas, La Reina and San Rafael. From La Laguna came the Sánchez family. An old man and his wife; their daughter, Luz; and her three children, the youngest of them an infant, strapped to her back with a black-threaded tapado. As they went along, she bounced lightly on the balls of her feet to produce a gentle jostle that lulled the baby into sleep. God forbid that he would start bawling and give them all away.

From Santa Rita came the two Velazco sisters and the six children they had between them. The family dog came, too, a curious-looking mutt with brown and white speckles. It trotted over the hills with its wet nose skimming the ground. One of the children, a five-year-old named Moisés, kept pace with the dog. It was his duty to shush the animal if it started to bark.

Still others called Las Vueltas and Vainillas and El Sitio their home. Adela Orellana and her ancient mother had spent the whole of their lives in this last place. As they lumbered along, Doña Carmelina used her crooked cane to steady herself. Both women wore their aprons, as if at any moment they would be called upon to cook.

Trudging over the land of their ancestors, land raped of topsoil and nutrients during indigo days, the people were oblivious to the toil of their forefathers, to the toll their labor had extracted from the earth. Yet the ancestral blood coursed through them and endowed them with strength and valor, and the grit to persevere. The people shored each other up as they plodded along. Those who could, balanced on their heads tubs filled with clothing and food and supplies. They carried rolled straw mats, cardboard boxes lashed with cord, baskets brimming with whatever was precious, with whatever they did not wish to leave behind to be sacked or destroyed.

Throughout the night, and over the next day, Nicolás placed one foot in front of the other, following Tata, who followed Basilio, who followed Paulina and Ursula and Delfina. Nicolás carried his machete. Hooked over his shoulder was his backpack. Inside the backpack rode the statue of la Virgen Milagrosa. Nestled against it was his mother's left shoe.

• • •

It was well after dusk when Nicolás's group arrived in La Arada. Like hundreds of others, they gave thanks that their long flight was almost over; that fate had delivered them safely thus far. They would spend the night near the river. At first light, they would cross over into Honduras. Thanks to Ursula's provisions, Nicolás and the other four ate their customary meal while huddled around their own little fire. Dozens like this flickered like fireflies over terrain dotted with shacks and stunted trees. The Sumpul River flowed gently beyond, below a steep bank choked with brush. The night felt close and the air hung heavy with impending rain—an unusual thing, for the start of the rainy season was yet half a month away. Still, all day, up and down the line, those who knew about such things pointed to the north, to the dark clouds boiling up over what they could see of the trees. "It's raining in Honduras," they said. The fact was worrisome, for rain, if copious, swept down the hills and caused the river to swell.

As he had throughout their journey, Tata put a question once again to Nicolás: "How's your side?"

"I need the bandage changed." Nicolás stated this matter-of-factly, but the truth was, he was frightened. His side ached dully, and at times he felt a stab of intense pain. He knew this did not bode well. He raised a hand to his brow and checked for fever, but his flesh was warm and not burning as he had feared. As for medical attention, he was now on his own. They had planned to stop at the clinic in El Carrizal, but before they reached it, they received the news that it had been destroyed. It was told that women working there had been raped and murdered. That the wounded had been finished off while lying helpless on their cots. Nicolás thought about el gringo Eddy. He hoped the doctor had left before the troops stormed in.

Nicolás dug in his backpack for the plastic bag with the medical supplies. His fingers touched the statue, and he laid a hand on it and said a little prayer: Virgencita, please don't let me get a fever. For added luck, he also touched his mother's shoe. He took out the bag and his flashlight, too, and handed the light to Basilio, who illuminated the area of the wound for Delfina. While she tended to him, Nicolás fixed his eyes on the wound. Though it ached, it did not look infected. He thought about crossing the river, remembering what Eddy had once told the old fisherman with the wormy leg sore: "Stay out of river water. River water's dirty."

"How high's the river here, Tata?" When they had arrived, it was too dark to slide down the bank and reconnoiter.

"Not too high."

"But how high? Will the water come up to my waist?"

"Maybe to your thighs. But don't worry, you know how to swim." Nicolás nodded and said no more.

Delfina turned her face up to Nicolás. The angled beam of the flashlight turned her face into a bizarre black-and-white mask. "There it is. Good for another day." Basilio switched off the light.

Nicolás thanked Delfina, gathered the supplies, and replaced them in the plastic bag. Then he remembered the cookies Our Holy Mother had given him. "I have dessert," he said, and passed them around.

Ursula gave a little cry of surprise when she got hers. "I think these are my favorite," she said. "Turn the light back on so I can see."

Basilio shined the light down on the cookie.

"It is my favorite!" Ursula said. "See? It says right here."

Nicolás peered down at the flat round disk. Imprinted on it was its maker's trademark: GALLETAS MARIA.

thirty-five

In mid-afternoon the army arrived in force. Rolling up in troop trucks and armored vehicles, it methodically deployed a battalion of men along a mile and a half stretch of the ridge overlooking the Sumpul. Joining them were units of the Guardia from Chalatenango and heavily armed squads from the paramilitary group Orden. For the moment, they stayed below the ridgeline, out of sight of the multitude gathered at the river's edge. They would not attack today. They would wait until morning. Then they would pounce on these communists insurgents, for that was surely what they were. Why else would they be fleeing? If they were good honest citizens, they had nothing to fear and would have stayed in their homes. Since they were not, they would pay the price that traitors always pay. It was the price of preserving a nation from the usurpers of the left, those dupes of Havana and Moscow. In the morning, another battle would be won and the country would take another cleansing step toward peace.

As darkness descended, Private José Delgado looked down on the valley from his vantage point on the ridge and saw the campfires of the enemy burning through the blackness and pointing fingers of flame to their presence. They made detection easy.

Delgado turned back to join his fellow soldiers and finish his suppertime rations: canned meat and vegetables, fruit cocktail, and tomato juice. He and four other soldiers had found a good spot for themselves under a tall shaggy pine. The tree had dropped many needles, and José rubbed a cluster of them between his fingers to scent his hand. He remembered when he was young he had traveled to the area frequently with his family. He had grown up in La Unión, a seaside port, hot and humid and smelling of fish and salt. His grandmother lived in Las Vueltas, hardly three kilometers from here, and his family had come regularly to enjoy the piney cool breezes of the north.

"It feels like rain," Delgado said to the others. He tilted his head up and sniffed the air. He did this confidently, for it was dark, so his companions could not catch him doing what he had done since he was a boy. Roberto, his older brother, had nicknamed him "el perrito" because of his penchant for sniffing the air. Roberto liked to taunt him by whistling and saying, "Come here, little doggie."

"It might feel like rain," one of the soldiers said, "but the rainy season is still weeks away."

He was wrong.

• • •

Sixty kilometers across the river, in Guaritas, Honduras, it had been raining since noon. A long soaking rain that, at first, the thirsty earth eagerly drank up. But after dusk the rain began to pool and overflow steadily down the hills until it slipped like silk over satin into the river. About five in the morning, the rain dwindled in intensity and trucks crowded with Honduran soldiers thundered through the little town of Santa Lucía toward the Sumpul, fourteen kilometers away. Their mission: to prevent the thousands of Salvadorans camped across the river from invading their country.

The Honduran government held little sympathy for El Salvador and the turmoil taking place there. Indeed, it had only recently gone to war with its tiny neighbor over a disputed soccer game that had exploded into an international incident. Now, here was this mob at its gates. Communist troublemakers. They would gain no admittance. They would not cross the river. The army would see to this. It would set up a line of defense along its banks and turn back the rabble.

• • •

Nicolás crept away from the others who were sleeping around the ashy remains of their campfire. It was not yet dawn, so he used the flashlight to find his way down to the river. As he edged down the steep slope, he used his machete to slash at the undergrowth that threatened to trip or snag him. Now that he was at the water's edge, he waved the beam of light back and forth along its surface. He could not believe his eyes. It was just as it had been in his dream. The river was up; halfway under water, saplings and scrub leaned hard downstream. The current was running swiftly. He focused on a small branch bobbing in the water; in two blinks of an eye, it floated out of view. He switched off the light and stood there, both awed and stunned. It was true what Our Lady had warned of in the dream: they should not cross at this spot. If he stepped into the water, it would rise well above his waist. "Go downriver," she had said. "Go now."

Nicolás switched the light on again and scrambled up the slope, keeping to the path he had taken before. He did not know what time it was, but the inkiness of night had begun to turn the dull color of lead. He kept climbing. When he reached the top of the slope, he was out of breath. His side ached fiercely. He could feel the perspiration breaking above his lip. With the flashlight to guide him, he wove his way between the families nestled together on the ground. Here and there, a few had started a morning fire to warm their breakfast. As he stepped around one group, his light shone on the face of a boy who looked like little Mario, the guerrillera nurse's son. The boy was awake. Amazingly, he did not startle when the light beam caught him. He was lying against his mother and made not a sound.

It took longer than Nicolás expected to find Tata. At one point he stumbled upon a group he thought was his, but then he realized his mistake and backed away, begging their pardon. When he did find his own people, he snapped off the light and dropped down beside his grandfather. Gently, he shook his shoulder. "Wake up, Tata, wake up." He spoke quietly for he did not wish to alarm the others. His grandfather sat up sleepily and struggled to a sitting position and looked around him. "What is it, boy?"

"The river's up, Tata."

"What?"

Now Basilio, lying close to Tata, sat up, too. "¿Qué pasa?"

"The river's up," Nicolás repeated. "Not only that, the current is swift."

"It *did* rain in Honduras," Basilio said.

Ursula woke up, and so did the other two women. "What's he saying?" Ursula mouthed the words around a long yawn.

"He said the river's up," Basilio replied.

"¡Uy! How high is it?" Ursula asked.

"At least up to my shoulders." To better make his case, Nicolás added a few inches.

"¡Uy! I can't get across when the water is up to there," Ursula said. "I can't swim."

"What are we going to do?" Delfina asked. "I can't swim either."

Paulina said nothing; she was simply another bundle huddled in the gloom.

Nicolás said, "We have to find a place where the river is wider and the water is not as deep."

"There's a place like that about a mile downstream," Tata said. "God knows this river is as familiar to me as the back of my hand."

"Let's go now, Tata."

"We don't have to go now," Ursula said. You could hear the stubbornness in her voice.

"Not right this minute, we don't," Delfina said. "Let's get the fire going and have a little coffee. I see others are starting to do the same. We have the morning to get across."

"No we don't," Nicolás said. "We have to go now." How could he explain the unexplainable? That he'd had a dream? That Our Holy Mother had told him what to do?

"Why do we have to go now?" Tata asked.

Nicolás leaned in close to his grandfather. He placed his face next to his and whispered in his ear: "Tata, it was la Virgen who told me." Nicolás could not see his grandfather, so he lifted his hand and lightly touched Tata's face. "It's true. She told me in my dream, Tata."

Tata said nothing for a moment, then he patted Nicolás's shoulder. "I think the boy has a point. We should get a head start. Once this crowd awakens, it's going to be bedlam."

Nicolás let out the breath he had not realized he had been holding. He pulled his backpack near and lashed it up and hooked it over his shoulder. The women grumbled their displeasure, but, still, they gathered up their things.

"You coming with us, Basilio?" Tata asked. He was already standing and putting on his hat.

"Why would I want to stay?" Basilio replied.

• • •

Tata led the way. Past the greater number of the people who were just coming awake. Past the friendly glow of their campfires. Past a few dogs that growled when they went by. They skirted clumps of trees and a half dozen shacks. Inside some of them, candles glowed. Soon other people materialized in the dawning light. It appeared that they, too, were getting an early start. The things they carried were great crowns resting on their heads. As they crossed paths, they nodded to each other. "Buenos días," they all said.

When there were no more shacks, Tata took a path trampled into a shine. The river ran to their left, beyond the ruff of tall sharp grass and down from a hill more gently sloped than the one upstream. In the burgeoning light, the ghostly mist rising from the water showed itself. To their right, the terrain flattened out. Here and there it cropped up into short hills, some dusted green with overgrowth, some bare with river-sculpted ledges and shelves.

Tata switched off the flashlight and handed it back to Nicolás. Nicolás stopped for a moment to open his bag and slide the flashlight into his mother's shoe. He slipped the pack on again and trotted painfully to catch up. Their line had rearranged itself. Now Tata was last, then Basilio in his Panama hat. Then the three women walking side by side. The six trudged on. Five minutes. Ten. The things making up the world around them—the mist, the brush, the hills, the path, the rocks and pebbles upon it—were struck by the sun and came fully into view. The world filled up with sound. The madrigal of birds. Perplexingly, a far-off refrain from a radio. And always, the steady murmuring sound of the river.

Nicolás moved toward the river and gave the brush a few whacks with his machete. He stared at the water. The mist was evaporating, and it was plain to see that the river was running fast. Here, too, it looked deep. He looked back toward the place where earlier he had stood in the dark. Already people were knotted along the bank there. Some stepped into the water and started across. He thought he could see the ruffles their little kicks made as they swam.

He had almost reached Tata again when rifle fire shattered the morning calm. For an instant, there was silence. In that moment, even the river went mute. Then more gunfire resounded from the hills above. Answering volleys from below melded with it. The women dropped what they were carrying. "¡Virgen Santa!" Ursula exclaimed.

Tata and Basilio turned toward the racket. The gunfire stopped. Delfina said, "Maybe that's all there was to it," but before she could say more a loud, low-pitched reverberation filled the air and two helicopters swept over the top of the ridge. The copters' waist doors were thrown open, and gunners, held fast in halters, squeezed the triggers on their side-mounted machine guns. Fire rained down on the people.

Basilio cried out, "Let's take cover!"

Tata pointed up ahead and off to the right. "That ledge over there!"

Ursula dashed up the path, then turned around and rushed back. "Not there! We have to get across!"

"The ledge is safer," Tata yelled, his voice swallowed up

by the roar of the helicopters and the gunfire and the screams and shouts of the people upriver. Some held on to their belongings. Others held tight to children, dragging them along. Some lifted young ones into their arms and ran ungainly on. The majority veered and crashed through the brush and scrambled down toward the water. Without looking back, Ursula and the women ran to join them.

Nicolás, Basilio, and Tata stayed together. The ledge was ahead, a haven from the flat terrain that now exposed them. The three scrambled up the slight incline. They focused on what was under their feet and not on what whirred above their heads. When they reached the ledge, Nicolás cast his backpack aside, the men their hats. Tata and Nicolás grasped their machetes. To fit under, the three hunched down low and pressed together. Once concealed, no one spoke. The only sound that came from them was their loud ragged breathing.

The world had gone mad. Tucked under the ledge, they witnessed everything. They saw the graceful swerves of the helicopters as they dipped over the people's encampment, as they swooped over the river and then swept back again. They saw the smoky lines of tracers tracking down running, panicked families. A mother holding a baby, the father in a straw hat, had almost made it to the top of the river slope when the bullets propelled them into heaps of blood and bone.

Under the ledge, Basilio said, "When I was a boy, I saw my family die like that." Nicolás turned his face to him and saw Basilio's dark lonesome eyes glistening.

From the hills now came the clamor of machine gun fire. They watched the people scatter in all directions and the dust rise in puffs around their stampeding feet. Even over the roar of the helicopters, they could hear the people's frantic pleas,

their wild laments. They saw people cascading down the incline toward the water. As they bumped and slipped along,
they mowed down the brush as if they were machetes; they
dislodged stones and dusty earth; they twisted arms and legs;
they broke their bones.

Pressed together under the ledge, Nicolás, Basilio, and
Tata saw the river churn with the frenzied movement of humanity struggling for their lives. They heard a fresh fusillade
of gunfire, and it came from a new direction: Honduran soldiers lined along the opposite bank were targeting the people
as they swam toward them.

Concealed under the ledge, outraged and incredulous,
they heard shooting from the right, from the left, and from
above. They watched the bullets find their marks. They
watched the people sink. They watched the river bury them.

Under the ledge, the three witnessed what their memories
would contain forever: River. Stone. Dust. Bone. These were
the things they would carry. The things they would not
forget.

thirty-six

After the helicopters made their last pass over the river and sped back to the base, after the troops ceased firing and the men shouldered their rifles and hiked back to the trucks, the Guardia swarmed down the ridge and rounded up those who were still alive, those unfortunates who had not managed to filter through to safety between the bullets of two armies. The people formed lines again, but not of their own choosing; their thumbs were lashed behind their backs with twine. Prodded by rifles, the people were marched away to be interrogated and jailed. Some, of course, were fated for worse.

Before the Guardias descended, and taking advantage of the unnatural stillness, Nicolás, Tata, and Basilio crept from under the ledge and scrambled to higher ground. Sheltered by pines and the tangle of underbrush, they hiked down the spine of a low ridge running parallel to the river. While crammed together under the ledge, they had laid out a plan: they would follow the ridge, veering south until the river turned a horse-shoe bend. They would go on to Las Vueltas, where one of Don Enrique Salah's candle factories was situated. Once there, Basilio would call his employer and Don

Enrique would come to fetch them. While they waited, Prudencio Murillo, the factory administrator, would see to their care. That was the plan.

But for now they walked abreast, Basilio in the middle. Alert and wary, they walked cautiously. Each held a weapon at the ready: Tata and Nicolás their machetes, Basilio a.38-caliber Smith and Wesson revolver. They seemed to be alone. But they took no chances. They communicated only by the wave of a hand or the tilting of a head. Their ears strained to catch the sound of a bootfall or the racheting click of a rifle. Their eyes sharpened toward each subtle change of light; their ears were keen to unexpected movement.

Though it was surely close to noon, it was not as sweltering because of the cloud cover. The sun poked weakly through the trees, creating spare and scattered shadows. Birds flitted about, and a few times their scuttlings caused the three to stop abruptly and stare hard. As they walked, Nicolás looked directly ahead and away from the river flowing at the foot of the hill to his left. He did not want to see it. He did not want to see the human cargo its swift waters carried: here an old man or a woman, there a child, and then, perhaps, its mother floating by.

They had been walking for an hour when the ridge turned to the right and dropped gradually down to the river. Nicolás hiked up the backpack resting between his shoulders. Our Lady at his back was a firm hand keeping him upright. His wound burned now, and he feared that it was bleeding. He could feel the moisture soaking through his shirt and around the side of his jeans.

"Can we stop for a moment?" he asked, breaking the silence they had maintained.

"I think it's safe," Tata said. As he had done many times during the flight, he passed a hand over his head, then let it drop. He had left his hat behind (as Basilio had), and he was obviously disturbed by its absence.

"Tata, see if I'm bleeding." Nicolás lifted his shirt. He did not look down. His face was hot, but he would not raise a hand to it. Two days had passed since he had been shot. If he had a fever now and he was bleeding, it would be the end of him.

Basilio poked his pistol into his waistband, and both he and Tata bent their heads to inspect the wound. "You're not bleeding," Tata said at length.

Nicolás lifted his arm and looked down at himself. The gauze circling him was grimy and soaked with sweat, but it was true. There was no blood. He lowered his shirt, feeling suddenly giddy. Already he felt cooler.

Basilio looked around. "Do you know where we are?" he asked Tata. "How far to Las Vueltas?"

"Maybe another hour—"

Before he could say more a loud flapping came from the tree directly above them. The sound startled them. Basilio laid a hand on his pistol. Tata took a step back. Nicolás ducked his head. The flapping started again. In unison, they looked up.

"¡Uy, zopes!" Nicolás exclaimed.

Two buzzards had settled like black statues upon a high limb of a dead pine.

"I hate zopes," Nicolás said.

Tata turned in a circle. He said, "Where there's zopes . . ."

Basilio pointed with his pistol beyond a clump of brush ahead. The three crept toward it. What met their eyes revolted them: perhaps a dozen buzzards sitting on the ground.

They flapped their wings and lunged and leaped. Several were perched directly upon what appeared to be three bodies. You could see their boots. The trousered legs. The birds extended their long wrinkled necks. With sharp powerful beaks, they dug into flesh. As they feasted, they swiveled their heads threateningly toward others attempting to partake.

For Nicolás, the sight of such horror threw a switch in his mind. He lifted his machete and raised his free hand and made a claw. Once again, he was a lion. He charged around the shrubbery. He lunged and growled. He leapt and hissed. The buzzards rose up in an explosion of flapping wings. Nicolás lashed out with his knife at their departing talons. Some swooped off across the river, others lit on the bare branches of pines. They pulled in their wings. Arranged themselves. Patiently, they waited.

Panting, Nicolás bent over. Hands on his knees, he propped himself up. Tata came to his side. He lay a calming hand on the nape of Nicolás's neck. "Hijo, hijo," Tata said. "Son, son." A reassuring murmuring.

After a moment, Basilio said, "Look at this."

Nicolás straightened up and turned his eyes on what Basilio held. It was an M-16 rifle. Like those Nicolás had seen with the guerrillas. Like those he had seen the soldiers carry.

"Where was it?" Nicolás asked, incredulous.

"Under one of the bodies." Basilio did not point, and not one of them looked. "That's three guerrilleros come upon bad times over there," he said.

"What are we going to do with that?" Tata asked.

Nicolás pulled the weapon from Basilio's hands. "I know what to do."

Nicolás walked over to the river's edge. He squatted down. Just as he had seen the soldiers do on so many nights as they sat cleaning their rifles after dinner, as he had watched them do at the firing range, he dismantled the rifle. His fingers were deft and he worked quickly.

First, he pressed the magazine release spindle and popped out the cartridge clip. Not surprisingly, there were no cartridges in it. He laid the clip down. He unscrewed the slip ring. One fast turn. Two. Then a third. When the barrel gave way, he laid it beside the clip. Next, he pressed the disconnect beside the trigger and the stock slipped loose. He set the stock beside the barrel. In his hands now lay the exposed firing chamber, that little mechanism of destruction.

He stood and gathered up the parts. He trotted a few paces downstream. Then he cocked his arm and hurled the firing chamber as far as he could. Then the cartridge clip as well. The stock and the barrel called for different measures. He twirled each over his head and flung when the momentum was right. He watched, first the barrel and then the stock, sail out over the water. He watched the splash each made as the river swallowed it up.

"Vaya," Nicolás said. He trotted back to Tata and Basilio. Both stood beside the river, their mouths agape.

"Vámonos," Nicolás said. "Let's go." He smiled shyly, turned away, and began walking again toward Las Vueltas and Don Enrique Salah's candle factory. He walked with the might of a lion, with the heart of a lamb.

EPILOGUE

From *La Prensa Gráfica*, May 25, 1999, San Salvador, El Salvador:

Dr. Nicolás de la Virgen Veras is the recipient of the prestigious Premio Manuel Quijano Hernandez, named after the noted physician, poet, and writer. The prize is granted yearly to a physician beginning his career who most exemplifies Dr. Hernandez's lifelong concerns for the needs of the Salvadoran people. Dr. Veras graduated with highest honors from the University Evangélica in 1996, where he attended the school of medicine. He recently finished a three-year residency specializing in traumatology with the Salvadoran Institute of Social Services, the ISSS. A reception in the Salón José Matías Delgado at the University Evangélica followed the prize-giving ceremony. Dr. Veras was honored by family and friends. Among them were his wife, Altagracia Veras, his grandfather, Celestino Veras; a longtime friend, Basilio Fermín; and his benefactors, Sr. don Enrique Salah and his wife, Sra. Florencia de Salah.

ACKNOWLEDGMENTS

I am indebted to Jim Kondrick, who lived this story with me every step of the way. Thank you, Jaimsey, for your love, for your keen eye, and for demanding the best that I can give. Also, my deepest appreciation and love to Anita Alvarez, Dr. Carlos Emilio Alvarez, and Jim Ables, who offered invaluable insights and assistance.

I am grateful to Ellen Levine, both friend and agent, and no better agent on earth; to Louise Quayle for her encouraging support; and to Leslie Wells for her editorial guidance and enthusiastic belief in my work. A special thank-you to Bob Miller for saying yes—one, two, three times.

And, as always, eternal gratitude to the Spirit without whom no words come. To la Virgen Milagrosa for the miracle of it.